Hobie Hanson
Greatest Hero of the Mall

JAMIE GILSON

Hobie Hanson
Greatest Hero of the Mall

Illustrated by Anita Riggio

Lothrop, Lee & Shepard Books
New York

Text copyright © 1989 by Jamie Gilson
Illustrations copyright © 1989 by Anita Riggio
All rights reserved. No part of this book may be reproduced or utilized in any form or by any means, electronic or mechanical, including photocopying, recording or by any information storage and retrieval system, without permission in writing from the Publisher. Inquiries should be addressed to Lothrop, Lee & Shepard Books, a division of William Morrow & Company, Inc., 105 Madison Avenue, New York, New York 10016. Printed in the United States of America.

First Edition 1 2 3 4 5 6 7 8 9 10

Library of Congress Cataloging-in-Publication Data
Gilson, Jamie. Hobie Hanson, greatest hero of the mall.
Summary: When his town is devastated by a flood, Hobie's fifth grade class is forced to meet every day in the shopping mall. [1. Floods—Fiction. 2. Shopping malls—Fiction. 3. Schools—Fiction] I. Title.
PZ7.G4385Hm 1989   [Fic]   89–2343
ISBN 0–688–08968–2

To the students
at Gurnee Grade School,
who told me wonderful stories

Contents

1. Monsters of the Deep

There's a fish in the backyard! Hobie! Come *see!*" Toby Rossi was calling me from the kitchen. "It's swimming around my swing!"

I was supposed to be baby-sitting Toby. Actually I was in the Rossis' family room sitting cross-legged in front of a coffee table, putting together a plastic see-through pumping heart. It was from this nine-dollar kit that has lots of tubes and little pieces and directions that don't make much sense. I was almost finished, checking over the final steps for about the tenth time because I didn't want to mess up.

"Hobie! It's swimming in *circles!*" The kid sounded pretty excited.

"Right," I called back.

Mrs. Rossi had taken Toby's big brother, Nick, to the dentist right after school. Nick, who's my best friend, had lost his only filling to a stick of licorice.

The TV behind me was set at superblast, the way Toby likes it. "So," I called over the noise, "you say a fish in the backyard is pumping your swing? I bet it just got out of school."

On TV the music turned scary. A cartoon bear on a raft was headed straight for the falls.

"Oh, no!" the bear moaned. He put his paws over his eyes.

"Oh, yes!" a fox snarled from the bank.

"Oh, wow," I said. I'd finally stuck all the plastic veins and arteries in the slots they were supposed to be stuck in. The tubes snaked around from points A to points B just as the Visible Pumping Heart directions said they should. I mean, I'd been working step by step on this model for three days, and it was practically perfect. You were supposed to hold the whole thing underwater in a bathtub to make sure it didn't leak, but I'd been so careful, that was one step I didn't need to take. Next, the directions said, you added blood.

It was phony blood, of course. You had to *make* it. But I was ready. I tore open a small paper packet and took out a dark red tablet, which I dropped into a cup of water. Nothing happened.

On TV the bear was swinging on a branch over the falls. A dog with a lasso was calling, "Stay right where you are."

"It's a *shark*!" Toby shrieked from the kitchen. He shrieks a lot. I think it's because he's four years old. "It's a real, live shark in my own backyard."

"Right," I called back, "a bloodthirsty shark." Setting the heart on its stand, I tuned the TV down to subnormal so I could think. The music had turned all happy, and the dog and the bear were standing on the bank watching the evil fox disappear down the foaming rapids.

"You're a hero," the bear told the dog. The dog smiled.

"Stay right where you are," I told Toby. "I'll be your hero." I smiled, too. Hero. It had a nice sound. And all I had to do was save Toby from bloodthirsty backyard sharks.

But first there was blood to make. Poking the pill around the bottom of the cup, I felt it crumble. The water turned tomato-juice red. So did my finger. To get the blood into the heart, the directions said, I had to disconnect the tubing from T-coupling 2.

"You're gonna miss it!" Toby yelled.

Now where was T-coupling 2? "That's a yard shark," I called. "For snacks it eats kids' toes. Whatever you do, don't try to pet it." Maybe that would keep him quiet a few minutes longer.

This plastic heart was important. It was my first science project for fifth grade. We were starting human body reports, and my name was on the list for tomorrow morning just after Nick's. He wouldn't tell what he was doing his report on. But whatever it was, he thought it was pretty funny.

Molly Bosco, who thinks she's the smartest kid in the world, was up just after me, doing her report on the brain. Figures. She'd probably made her model from scratch instead of using a kit. She's a serious big-time show-off.

But mine would be world class. My heart had valves and ball bearings and blood. All you had to do, the directions said, was squeeze this little rubber bulb, and red dye would shoot through all the right spaces.

First, of course, I had to fill it, and that wasn't going to be easy. It took thinking. I couldn't fill my heart and play fish games with Toby at the same time.

"*Two* sharks!" he yelled. "Hobie, come quick! I see *two*!"

The kid has a wild imagination. Some of his best friends are dinosaurs.

He ran into the family room with an ice cream bar, its juice dripping down his arm. "Well, you missed it," he said, watching me pump fake blood into the heart. "The sharks swam away. They went to your yard." I squeezed the rubber bulb, and red rushed in veins and out arteries. *Lub dup.* It filled up chambers. I pressed again. *Lub dup.* And again. *Lub dup.* It was beautiful.

"Is it supposed to drip like that?" Toby asked.

Every time I squeezed the bulb, some of the red stuff oozed out the bottom and onto the coffee table.

"That's sick," he said, looking at the mess. He dropped the rest of his ice cream into the wastebasket I was using for scraps. "You know what? That's really sick."

"Thank you," I told him, holding the drip of red stuff back with my fingers.

He poked a button on the TV and changed the channel. "You're finished, Scumbreath," a guy snarled. *ZAP. BOOM. BOP.*

Outside, in the distance, thunder rolled on and on.

"It's raining like crazy," Toby said, tugging the sleeve of my sweater, "Scumbreath."

"Don't call me Scumbreath. That's not nice." Toby's mom really spoils him. "In case you haven't noticed," I told him, "rain is nothing new. It's been raining like crazy for ten days now."

The rain didn't worry me. What worried me was that I had a broken heart and a lot of fake blood on my hands. Where did I mess up? I was so sure I'd done everything right. Maybe the blood was dissolving the glue. Somehow I had to figure out how to drain the heart without getting red stuff on the rug. The directions said the dye would stain.

"Where did the sharks come from?" Toby asked, pulling again at my sleeve. "I never saw them before."

"They fell from the sky with the rain," I explained. "They are sharks that grant wishes. You know the kind. 'Magic fish, magic fish, grant my wish, grant my wish.' "

"Hummm." He was thinking. "Like wishing for diamonds?"

"More like wishing to stay up late." The drip

was still dripping. I turned the heart upside down.

"Those sharks. They don't *steal* diamonds, do they?" he asked. "I mean, they're not *bad* sharks."

"Well, you don't read much about big-time fish thieves," I told him, "but I have heard that sharks are very greedy."

"Then I better make sure our diamonds are safe," he said, heading out of the room.

The kid was finally going to let me alone. "Great idea," I called after him. "Check on the rubies, too. And the emeralds."

I took the gum I was chewing out of my mouth, divided it in half, and plugged up two of the main leaks. Even upside down, the heart kept dripping.

"Toby!" I yelled. "Would you bring me a bowl or something to dump this fake blood in?" Where was he when I needed him? "Hurry!"

After about forever, he appeared at the door with this huge roasting pan, big enough to hold a turkey. He sat it at my feet.

"You're welcome . . . Scumbreath," he said, giggling.

I growled.

He grabbed a Mighty Mouse knapsack out of the pan and flopped on the sofa. Hugging the knapsack close, he leaned his cheek against Darryl, his stuffed stegosaurus.

"I wished on the fish," he said after a while.

Lightning cracked somewhere close.

"I wished for my mommy and Nick." His bottom lip looked fat and it began to shake. I hate it when little kids cry.

"They'll be back soon," I told him. "The dentist doesn't want Nick any more than Nick wants the dentist." I set my heart model in the pan and watched it drip around the gum. So much for world-class reports.

Toby clicked the remote control, changing from station to station, but cartoons were over for the afternoon. That meant it was five o'clock. Nick and his mom should have been home half an hour ago. At least.

"Thursday, October twenty-sixth, and stormy weather leads off our local news," the anchor in the blue dress said, smiling. "Yesterday our main man meteorologist *promised* us there'd be *no more rain*." She turned to the fat guy next to her. "Don," she scolded

9

him, "you tricked us again. You said that storm would pass us by." Then she forgave him with a smile. "Don has a fabulous forecast for tomorrow, though. Sunny skies will light up our lives.

"But today," and her sad face already told the story, "many places, already hard hit, have had five more inches of rain—all in the last two hours. The Hawk River in some spots has broken over its banks. Widespread flooding is reported in northern sections where residents are warned to—"

Pop. The lights went out. *Poof.* The anchorperson in blue and the happy weather guy dissolved like wet sugar.

"Hey, Tobe," I said, remembering his shaky lip, "no big deal, OK? Power just blew. They fix things like that by climbing a pole. OK? Trust me, Hobie H. Hero." I beat my chest with my fists like an ape.

"You lied about the sharks," Toby said, digging his fist into Darryl.

Little kids can't tell the difference between playing games and telling lies. "Why do you think that?" I asked him.

"My mom and Nick aren't home, that's why.

And I wished two times, one for each shark. You *said*. Besides, you're as scared as I am." He snuffled. "Some hero."

I stood up, grabbed his arms, and lifted him off the couch. Thunder was rumbling, and so was I, but no little kid was going to catch me scared. "Let's you and me attack the kitchen," I told him, highly happy, as if we were talking balloons and circuses. "We'll sing silly songs and pop a bag of corn."

"No we won't." He wiggled free. "The microwave is dead. It plugs in."

He may be four, but he's not dumb. "Well, let's go, anyway. I'll call the electric company."

In the kitchen we stared out the window through sheets of rain blowing sideways. The water *was* deep. When we came home from school, you could see the Rossis' grass and my grass next door. Now the seat of Toby's swing was hopping on top of waves.

"Look." Toby pointed. "Our picnic table's floating. And it's pea green. Maybe we could go to sea in it like the Owl and the Pussycat." He began to giggle again.

Through slaps of rain you could just make out the long green table and its benches,

11

rocking free next to the back fence. It did look like the kind of bizarre boat the Owl and the Pussycat might have hung out on.

Cupping my hands around my eyes, I pressed my nose to the window and spotted, closer in, the top of the Rossis' barbecue grill. Its round, red lid poked out of the waves like an alien sub. Next to it something that looked a little like a carp flopped in the water. Probably, I decided, a loose skateboard.

"There it is! My shark!" Toby said, pointing again. "Did you see it?"

Lightning cracked the sky. Twice. I'd read somewhere that lightning can shoot through telephone wires, and while I hadn't heard Molly's report yet, I figured one long zap ear to ear could fry your brain in a big way. I decided to forget the phone. Who would I call, anyway? The electric company didn't need me to tell it the lights were out. Since it was after five, both my mom and my dad would be on their way home from work. Besides, I didn't want them to know I was scared of a little noise.

Thunder shook the kitchen dishes. Twice. I closed my eyes and swallowed hard.

"Hobie," the kid said, "what's the name of our river?"

"It's the Hawk. You know that," I told him with a big fat fake laugh, as if it was the punch line to a joke. The Hawk's not exactly ours, but it runs along about five blocks from our houses. Nick and I go there to skip stones, and to fish sometimes.

"Is it the same Hawk the lady said on TV?"

"Yeah, she said it was high. Those guys who live near it are probably getting wet."

I looked out the kitchen window. The rain was slowing down. You could see better. The skateboard flopping in the waves didn't have wheels. It had fins, at least one eye, and a tail. Toby's fake shark was a real live river carp.

My dad had told Mom and me just the night before that the sandbags piled along the banks of the Hawk would keep it from flooding. He said that even if the Hawk *did* overflow, it would never ever reach our house. It never had before and it never would. He *said*. But that fish sure hadn't fallen from the sky to grant wishes. It had swum there. And the only place it could have swum from was the Hawk River. In the two hours since school let out, the Hawk had washed over its banks. Outside was a lake. And inside, the rooms were sinking in blue-gray shadows.

I wanted to be a hero, but I didn't feel brave. There was a storm in my stomach.

The night was going to take us over. "Where's a flashlight?" I asked Toby.

"In the basement, but I bet it's really really dark down there."

I figured that was true. Dark and getting darker. "Where's a candle?"

"On the dining room table, but I don't know about matches."

Me either, so I just stood and looked out the window at the water moving. Up.

"I'm scared of dark," Toby said.

"Being scared of the dark is kid stuff," I told him. I didn't point out that I was a kid, too.

"When is my mom coming home?"

"Soon," I told him. As soon, I thought, as she gets an outboard motor on her station wagon. The water out there was car-window high. It wasn't play water, either, for wading in or floating leaf boats on. That water would shove you under and hold you down.

"Hobie," the kid said, grabbing the leg of my pants. I tried to shake him loose. I was tired of his questions. I had a few of my own. Like *how* do heroes save the day? Or the night? I think light bulbs are supposed to go on in their heads. My head was having power failure.

"Hobie!" He was really bugging me. "I hear gargle monsters. I saw them once on TV. They have horns and wings and they sit on roofs and they throw up water when it rains. Listen."

I stood still and listened. I could hear my heart, *lub dup*. Do heroes hear their hearts beat?

I could hear something else, too. It wasn't the rain. The rain had almost stopped. I closed my eyes and listened harder. It didn't sound like a fake shark. Or a real carp. It sounded more like some mega-mad TV monster throwing back its head and gargling up a storm. But it couldn't be that. The TV was dead.

2. Knock Knock

I headed straight for the living room windows. Toby followed. When we looked out, it was weird. No lights were on. No cars were even trying to splash through. In the distance sirens whined. The sidewalk and the street had both disappeared. A purple Big Wheel with nobody on it was bobbing around where the street used to be.

Next door, my house looked empty, though I knew Fido was inside. She doesn't mind the dark. But I'd never seen her swim. Actually, I'd never won prizes for swimming, myself. I must have sucked in my breath.

"What's the matter? You scared we're gonna drown?"

The thought had crossed my mind. Tom Sawyer almost got drowned in a flood. On TV sometimes, too, I've seen people holding on to chimneys in floods, and I've seen dogs caught on the peaks of roofs. Never cats.

"Drown? I'd never let us do that. Let's get some peanut butter and jelly so I can think." I hurried him back toward the kitchen. In the hall, as we passed the basement door, I heard a knock and bump, but the sounds were too soft to be monsters. Besides, monsters don't exist. Maybe it was the wind, though mostly there isn't wind in basements. I walked faster. My heart began to pump as though something inside me was squeezing a bulb to the beat of loud, fast music. *Lub-dup-lub, lub-dup-lub.*

With shaky hands I piled PB and J on graham crackers for Toby. Thunder growled and lightning struck inside my stomach. I wasn't hungry. Don't, I thought—whatever you do—don't let the kid know you're scared.

"Hey, Tobe, how about if we give your dad a call?" I said, bright as a two-hundred-watt bulb. "Sometimes he works late. We'll tell him we're surrounded by sharks, the picnic table's loose, and my cat's at home by herself. Then maybe he'll, you know, head right home."

17

Toby's dad's number was on the list taped to the wall. I could just make it out in the half dark. So what if he laughed at me.

The lightning had stopped for the time being, so I figured I could call without getting scrambled brains. I picked up the phone with two fingers and pushed 8-2-2. Nothing zapped my ear. Nothing at all. The buttons didn't even make friendly little *boop beep beeps*. I might as well have been talking to a banana. What I had in my hand was a stone-dead telephone.

Toby stood still, waiting.

"Nobody there," I told him, not exactly lying. Phones don't just stop working in storms. Something must really be wrong. "Probably he's on his way," I explained. Then it hit me. Toby's dad wasn't going to make it unless, just to be wacky, he'd carried a canoe to work.

When I closed my eyes to think, all I could see clearly was deep water.

"Why is the basement monster making that funny noise?" Toby asked. "Is it throwing up? Does it have fangs? Are you still scared?"

"Monsters," I explained, "are just pretend. They are in books and TV and movies, not under beds or in basements. Even very dark basements." That's what my mom used to tell me when I was little. I didn't believe a word of it.

Knock knock. A real something was thumping on the basement door. *Knock knock.*

"Who's there?" I called. My voice sounded as though I'd just drained a helium balloon. The only answer was another *knock knock.*

"Is it after us?" Toby asked.

"It's not after us," I told him, looking around for a place to hide.

"Maybe it needs help," Toby said.

"Nothing's down there," I explained, which was a dumb thing to say because something was knocking.

"Are we scared to look?" Toby asked.

"OK, you want to look, we'll look," I told him. I did not want to look. I did not want to meet a fictional beast.

Still, we padded quietly down the hall to the basement door. The rug felt spongy. The door shook. *Knock knock.*

Toby hid behind me. "Let's forget it," he whispered.

Good idea, I thought, but I couldn't back

down now. "Trust me," I said, and I slowly turned the knob to show the kid how brave I was. I meant to open the door just a crack, but when it clicked free, it pushed itself wide against us. And as we jumped back, a splash lapped over the top step and onto our feet.

Toby yelped and pulled my T-shirt longer. I grabbed him and pressed us both against the hall wall. From the dark hole of the basement, the river flood swept out a five-part monster that wasn't like any I'd ever imagined. Knocking at the door to scare the pants off us both was one Ping-Pong paddle, two balls, a bottle of bleach, and a long-handled broom.

I laughed so hard I almost cried.

"It smells like somebody wet his pants," Toby said, holding his nose.

It did, too. I bet real monsters don't smell any worse. The stink meant the sewer was backing up. Stuff was spewing in through the toilet downstairs. The Hawk was spreading.

If we'd been at my house, we could have gone upstairs to higher ground, but the Rossis didn't have a second floor. We couldn't go up and we sure couldn't go down. Down was an indoor pool you wouldn't want to swim in. We couldn't stay where we were. The floor we were standing on was getting wetter. We could sit on tables for a while, maybe. Then the highest thing we'd be able to reach would be the hanging light in the dining room. But even if it held us both, when the power came back on we'd get grilled.

At home, my cat would go upstairs. Of course she would go upstairs. I was sure she would go upstairs. What if she didn't go upstairs? What if she was already in my basement, trying to dog-paddle?

I had to save Fido, too.

Tom Sawyer would have hopped on a raft to save his cat. I didn't have a raft and I didn't have any logs to build one with, though it was clear that brooms could float. And Ping-Pong balls.

"Hobie!" The kid was at my elbow again. "I found some matches in a drawer. You want them?"

I wanted them. I took them to the dining room to light the long white candles on the table. The first two matches didn't work, but I lit both candles with the third. The dining room glowed orange, almost as scary as black.

In the family room Toby yelped, and I nearly knocked him down as we both rounded the corner from opposite directions.

"You're not gonna believe this," he said, panting. "But I went back to the sofa to save Darryl and the diamonds, and you know what? Water is squirting out where the TV is plugged in."

Clearly he was lying. Of course he was lying. But then, I'd thought he was lying about the fish in the yard. I went to look.

Water *was* squirting out where the TV was plugged in. It was also squirting out where the lamp was plugged in. The waterfalls were making a lake of the family room.

This, I thought, is hero time. We're on a sinking ship. Right now is when I've got to save Toby, his stegosaurus, the see-through plastic heart, and my cat next door, who trusts me. I grabbed the turkey roaster with the heart in it and slogged wet-footed into the living room with Toby at my heels.

We sat on high-backed chairs and stared at each other. What to do? If I had a rope like the one the TV dog had, I could lasso the picnic table in the backyard. Then we could paddle it with a broom. Idea one.

Pow pow pow. Something was bashing the front door. *Pow pow.* This time the pounding wasn't a half-empty bottle of bleach. It was loud. I hadn't heard a motorboat roaring up to bring someone, but it sounded like a real person, kicking. A guy in trouble, maybe, who'd found out the hard way his car didn't float.

POWPOW.

"OK, OK," I called, running down the hall to the front door. Toby was at my heels.

When I got there, even though whoever it was was still kicking away, I turned the knob and pulled slowly, slowly, with my foot against the door, hoping the river wasn't over porch-high yet, waiting to knock us down.

When I peeked out the crack, I didn't believe what I saw.

It was Molly Bosco. Water from her yellow slicker sprayed us as she rushed into the house. When I slammed the door behind her, I saw she was clutching something tight. I looked closer, blinking.

"Fido?" I asked. "Is that Fido?" Maybe the water just *looked* deep. Maybe everything was all right. My cat was clearly alive. I almost hugged them both.

"What took you so long?" Molly asked.

Fido's ears were back and her tail was wet. I felt her shivering as I grabbed her.

"This is amazing," I said, hugging wet Fido. "How did you get here?" I knew Molly's parents were traveling someplace really far away, like Brazil. "You're not by yourself?"

She nodded. "My grandmother's playing bridge in Barrington, so nobody's home at my house. I knew you were here sitting Toby. I heard you talking to Nick after the math test. In fact, I heard you talking to Nick *during* the math test."

Molly hears all.

"How'd you get Fido?" I asked her.

"She was on your front porch," Molly said. "Crying. She came to me and snuggled on my shoulder."

"That can't be," I told her. "Fido doesn't go out in the rain. Also, she doesn't come to anybody but me and my mom."

Molly smiled. "She came to me."

"Did you swim here?" Toby asked her.

"Of course not. I got here by African animal." She grinned strangely.

She must be crazy scared, poor kid. "It's OK," I told her. "I'm working out an escape.

You can float away with us on the picnic table." I would be her hero, too. Already I was feeling much better. "Just come right over here and sit down on the sofa. Only its feet are wet. Everything is going to be all right."

She didn't sit down. "Of course everything is going to be all right," she told me. "I have a plan." She put one hand on Toby's shoulder and one hand on mine.

"I have come," she said, "in my inflatable giraffe, to rescue you."

3. Molly Bosco to the Rescue

What a stupid thing to do! Really amazingly stupid," I told her. "You live two blocks from here. You could have been grilled by lightning or drowned."

"Or eaten by sharks," Toby suggested.

Molly sighed to let us know we were terminal dumbheads. "Naturally I waited until the lightning and the rain had stopped. Then I pushed off."

"In your giraffe," I said, not believing this for a minute.

"In my giraffe."

"Where is it now?" Toby asked.

"I paddled it up to the porch, dragged it over, and wedged it behind the wicker chair, which wasn't easy because I was holding Fido."

"I want to see the giraffe," Toby said, opening the door. "They can't talk, you know. Giraffes can't."

"This one squeaks if you pinch its tail," Molly told him, "but it'll only hold two of us at a time. Come on, I'll show you." They splashed onto the porch.

I sat Fido on the sofa and told her to stay. Giving a long low hiss like a leaky tire, she leapt off toward Nick's bedroom.

"Wow," Toby said from outside. "This is *yours*? Lucky duck. Really yours? Can I have a ride? Can I have a ride right now?"

"Get your raincoat," Molly told him. "And bring that blanket thing you sleep with. Then I will personally save you from drowning and despair."

Sounded suspicious to me. I pushed open the screen door. The water it hit made waves. Off to the side, behind the big white wicker chair, Toby was sitting in a giraffe, the kind they pump up for little kids to splash around in. It was as tall as I am, only it had spots on its neck. And just as Molly had said, it was a two-seater. With oars.

"That's crazy," I told her. "This is a toy. I won't let Toby ride in it. I'm in charge of him. He's staying right here with me."

"Am not! You're finished, Scumbreath," Toby said as he climbed out of the giraffe and

headed into the candlelit house. "Wait for me, Molly."

"You are, *too*! And don't call me Scumbreath. He watches too much television," I told Molly. "Where'd you get this, anyway?" The giraffe didn't look, somehow, like the kind of thing Molly Bosco would have sitting around her room.

"It's from my childhood," she explained. "My grandmother gave it to me for my birthday when I was six years old. It's very big, really. It took fifteen minutes with a hand pump to fill."

"I never saw it before," I told her.

"That's because I've never used it here. The lifeguards wouldn't let me bring it in the pool. When I was young, I spent hours and hours rowing it during Lake Geneva vacations. People called me the giraffe girl."

Giraffe girl! Molly Bosco? "That thing's made of plastic," I pointed out. "It must have leaks. I can't believe you didn't sink straight down to the dandelions. This is crazy. No way you're going to take my kid anywhere in that thing."

"Hobie, this house is filling up with water. Right?" She was, of course, right. The porch water was cold on my ankles. It was true we had to leave. I knew we had to leave. The sirens were still on in the distance.

"I could make a boat out of the picnic table," I told her. "We could paddle it to high ground."

"Maybe," she said. "But you don't *need* to make a boat. I *have* a boat. Besides, I don't think a picnic table would be seaworthy. My boat is. I know, because that's how I got here."

I'd never actually seen anybody sail a picnic table. That was true. Water began to wash up on the porch. It was like a beach at high tide.

"It's practically dark," Molly said. "And what I've decided we've got to do is go to school."

"School? What'll we do there, study fractions?" She was going bonkers.

"School is where people stay when it floods. You see it all the time on the news. Whenever something awful happens in a town, people bring their blankets and sleep on the floor at school."

She'd worked it all out in her head. I'd never even thought about where to steer the green table. But I'd seen those pictures on TV, too. Kids racing around the gym.

The giraffe was starting to float on the

porch. My toes squished in my sneakers.

"Where is everybody?" I asked, looking across our river street at the dark, quiet houses.

"People are inside because their houses are islands and they can't get off. Everybody else is looking for boats. We have one."

"I'm not going anywhere in that giraffe."

"School's not all that far," she said. "First I'll take Toby. Then I'll come back for you. Don't worry. I am an expert rower."

"Here I am," Toby said, pushing open the door and sloshing across the porch. He had on red boots and a red raincoat. Besides Darryl, he was hugging an umbrella with a Donald Duck head and his baby blanket packed with treasures. He stuffed the whole thing in the giraffe.

Molly opened the blanket and began to toss stuff out onto the wicker chair. "The tow truck stays behind." She pitched it. "And so does GI Joe. You watch too much TV."

Toby rescued GI Joe. Then he snatched Darryl before Molly could and started to snuffle.

Snuffling didn't stop Molly. "The umbrella

might poke a hole. We'll leave it here. And take those boots off. They weigh a ton. Besides, your feet are already wet. OK, what's this?" She picked up the Mighty Mouse knapsack, reached in, and took out a small black box.

"You can't throw that away," Toby said, grabbing. Molly held the box over her head. "You *can't*. My mommy's diamond earrings are inside and they're brand-new and she would die if they drowned. I went in her room and saved them from the sharks." He began to wail.

"Sharks? Diamonds?" Molly asked, and started to open the box. Toby wrestled it from her and shoved it at me.

The box felt soft. Velvet. I flipped it open. Inside, clipped on shiny white satin, were two huge diamonds, as big around as jumbo olives. They sparkled like tiny blue light bulbs.

Molly sucked in her breath. "I didn't know your folks were *that* rich," she told Toby.

I didn't know the Rossis were rich at all, except sometimes my dad said they spent money like they had it to burn. But those diamonds looked as if they'd burned up whole bonfires of bucks.

Toby wailed louder.

"Don't be a dolt, Toby. I won't throw them away," Molly said. She put her hand out. "I'll keep them perfectly safe."

I snapped the box shut and held the diamonds behind me. "You might lose them in the water. *I'll* keep them safe. Look, why don't we all just stay here and wait? Somebody's bound to come."

"No way!" she said, and towing the giraffe by the neck, she dragged it to the top of the steps. "Toby," she told him, "stop crying and get in." He did both. He sat where she told him to, in the back seat facing the neck of the giraffe. In a python grip he held GI Joe, the stegosaurus, and his blanket. His bare feet were resting on two big silver flashlights.

"I brought two lights because I thought you might need one," Molly said, handing her extra to me. "We'll turn ours on for a headlight. You can use yours to keep you company."

How could she tell I was scared? My hands were hardly shaking. I'd have given her back the light, but it *was* getting darker and darker, and the Rossis' flashlights were shipwrecked on the floor of their basement sea.

Molly got into the boat facing Toby. She grabbed the oars, which were held by rubber loops to the giraffe's sides.

"Push off!" she ordered, like the captain of a ship, and I gave the giraffe a good swift kick from behind to set it free from the porch. Its long neck swayed side to side as the boat hit open water.

"Stop wiggling," Molly said, rowing over the lawn. Toby turned and flashed the light in my eyes. It was eight blocks to Central School and she couldn't even see where she was going. To row the giraffe forward, she had to face its tail. What if she hit a lamp post? Or a stop sign? In the distance sirens were still groaning. This was a bad idea. I knew it was a bad idea.

"Don't go!" I called.

"Now, Hobie, no need to be afraid," Molly said. "I'll be back before you know it. Keep dry. Don't open the door to strangers. And, whatever you do, don't lose those earrings. They're worth a fortune." The boat skimmed across the water. "Have a nice day!" she called.

If Toby hadn't been in the giraffe, I'd have waded out and pulled its plug.

4. The Hissing Panther Pillowcase

Two eyes glowed in the dark. I lay on my damp belly staring at them.

"Monster," I said, "here's monster meat. Yum yum. Come and get it."

Fido was under Nick's bed. I slid under, too, the floor around me soggy from the rising water. It was a dumb place to be. I knew it was a dumb place. But then I was feeling dumb. The time had come for me to save the day, to make things right when everything, *everything*, was going wrong, and instead I let Molly come and take my kid away in a plastic giraffe. The very least I could do was save Fido.

I had stood outside on the porch calling her, but she didn't come. While I was calling, I saw a rowboat go by low in the water with a man and woman and kid in it holding suitcases and a TV. They asked me if I was OK and I lied and said yes. But what if they'd rowed over and I'd gotten in and then Molly had come back for help and I wasn't there?

Back into the spooky house was not where I wanted to go. But I had to. Fido was inside and so was my heart.

Some hero I'd turned out to be.

Scrunching farther under the bed, I pointed the flashlight at the tip of the cat's tail so as not to scare her. Under my arm I'd tucked a panther-striped pillowcase, in which I planned to capture friend cat. In the other hand I held a bowl full of tuna fish.

Not having cats, the Rossis didn't have any real cat food, so I'd opened a can of tuna packed in oil.

I pushed the bowl ahead of me. Fido was hiding out behind a tennis shoe, a pile of dirty socks, and a stack of library books.

"Here, kitty-kitty," I called, sticking the tuna almost under her nose. She turned her head away. She knew it was fish, all right, but, no dummy, she also knew it was a trap.

Being nice wasn't working. No more Mister Good Guy. "Come out right now, you bad beast! Or I'll pull you out by the tail."

I aimed my light at her yellow eyes and crept deeper under the bed until my head just hit the middle springs.

Pushing the tuna slowly, slowly forward, I got myself all set to grab her with my free hand and stuff her in the king-sized pillowcase, when she unwound suddenly like a spring and leapt out into the dark.

I rested my forehead on the soggy rug. Fido's a nice cat and all that, but not under a bed with ancient dirty laundry, soggy fuzz balls, and rejected fish. I growled. Fido circled around, lay down on my right leg, and began to purr.

POW POW. Somebody was pounding on the front door. Molly couldn't possibly have made it to school and back. Raising my head fast, I banged it on the slats. *POW POW.* I'd locked up and chained the door so looters couldn't get in to steal Mrs. Rossi's mammoth diamonds.

Fido ran. *POW. POW. POW.* When I grabbed for the flashlight, my hand hit the edge of the tuna bowl. It spun, tipped, and spilled tuna in a wet heap just under my neck. As I slid out, a trail of fishy oil dripped from my chin.

"What took you so long?" Molly asked when I opened the door a crack and peeked through. She wasn't alone. I pulled the door wider. A teenage-type girl was with her.

"Where's Toby?" I asked, searching the dark behind her. But he wasn't there. She'd lost him. I knew she'd lost him.

"We'd only gone a block or so before we ran into R. X. Shea," Molly said, "and his sister, what's-her-name."

"I'm Heidi," the girl told me, stepping inside. "My brother and I got our rowboat out from the garage to save people." R.X. is this kid in fifth grade with us. I didn't even know he *had* a sister.

"I told them you needed saving," Molly said, patting my arm. "So we turned back." Then she held her nose and took two steps away. "What have you been *doing*?"

"Hurry *up*!" Toby yelled from outside. By squinching my eyes, I could just make out a real boat sitting practically on the front porch. Toby and R.X. were in it.

"Hey, Hobie," R.X. called. "Is this something or what? Mom's out picking people up in our canoe."

Fido was trying to climb my leg.

"Here, hold this open wide," I told Molly, handing her the panther pillowcase. And, peeling Fido off my jeans, I stuffed her inside.

"Hold up a second," I told them. Swinging the cat sack by my side, I dashed to the dining room, blew out the candles, and grabbed the black plastic garbage bag that I'd filled with two important things—my heart for tomorrow's report and, of course, Mrs. Rossi's diamond earrings. I slipped the bag's drawstring over my wrist, told Fido everything was going to be all right, and ran back through the dark hall.

"You smell bad," Toby said, holding his nose as I sloshed across the porch. I guess he could tell from that far away. "You sit someplace else."

"Grrrrrrrrr," something in the boat growled. Either Toby was turning mean or there was a passenger I couldn't see.

"My dog," R.X. explained, "doesn't much like cats."

From inside the pillowcase Fido hissed. "My cat," I told him, "doesn't much like dogs, either. But I can't leave her here. She'd drown for sure."

"RRRRrrrrrrrr." The small brown poodle in

R.X.'s arms strained to get free, its engine running on high.

"I don't think they want to sit together," Molly said. She wrinkled her nose. "Look, Hobie, why don't you just ride back in the giraffe. We'll tow you."

They'd tied a rope to a loop at the base of the giraffe's neck and attached the creature to the rowboat like a caboose. It was heaped with packages.

Heidi, who said she was worried about boat overload anyway, agreed. Either that or she didn't want to ride in the same space with a kid who smelled like tuna oil and rug fuzz.

So I gave R.X. and Molly the stuff that was in the giraffe to hold in their laps and climbed in with Fido, holding her pillowcase tight in my arms.

As the boat floated free, the dog howled. Fido yowled. The giraffe weaved from side to side on its rope the way drunks in movies do. When Heidi jerked the boat fast forward, I pitched back and the giraffe's tail squeaked. Toby began to cry.

"Off we go," Molly called brightly. I think she was having a good time. I know she was having a good time. As if it was "Mary Had a Little Lamb," she sang, "Off we go to Central School, Central School, Central School."

I felt seasick.

"Central School?" Heidi asked, huffing as she rowed. "Why would you want to go there?"

"Because that's where everybody *is*," I heard Molly explain to her, pointing her flashlight in the direction of the school. "That's where we'll sleep tonight. That's where the doughnuts are and the hot chocolate and the blankets."

Boats were beginning to pass us in the street, the people in them calling out to see if we were OK. They pointed and laughed at the giraffe. I scrunched down so nobody would recognize me.

"You *sure* you want to sleep at Central?" Heidi asked.

"Sure, I'm sure."

"We've been past there," R.X. told her. He turned around and aimed his flashlight beam at me. "You should see it. Heidi and me, we looked in the windows. You sleep there tonight and you'll be sleeping on a *real* waterbed."

"What do you mean by that?" Molly asked suspiciously.

"I'll tell you what I mean," R.X. said, his voice mysterious as if he was telling ghost stories. Another boat passed us, and its waves made the giraffe wobble and bounce. Heidi rowed faster. The deep gray dark turned darker. "We pulled up next to Central School in this boat less than one hour ago," he went on, "and we flashed our light in Mrs. Finn's room, that third grade near the front door. And you know what we saw? The water inside was really, really deep. It came halfway up the chalkboard. It was so deep that Mrs. Finn's desk was floating in the middle of the room. And you know what was on top of her desk? Her grade book was on top. Wide open. And you know what was on top of that?" He waited for us to guess, but since nobody did, he made his voice lower and went on. "On top of the grade book, crawling slowly across the page, was this great big fat red-eyed river rat. That's what."

Toby squealed.

I gagged. Then I caught my breath. And it wasn't just because Central School was drowning in water and crawling with rats. While I was listening to R.X.'s story, Fido was clawing a hole in the panther pillowcase. And she hadn't stopped there. She'd ripped through a layer of striped plastic. The giraffe began to hiss. Then it started to fold in around me, wrapping me tight and sucking me down—not fast, the way a rock would sink, but slow, like M&M's in a chocolate malt. The water was cold. It soaked through my jeans and my underwear and crept up my T-shirt.

I couldn't kick my feet free. I couldn't get Fido free either. She was caught tight in my lap, all tangled in the shreds of the pillow-case, a crazy cat, scratching. My jacket ballooned. The water rose to my armpits. In the rowboat everybody was talking loud about rats and river-up-to-the-chalkboard, and nobody was looking back at me.

The giraffe's nose bent down and touched the water. No way I was going to be able to kick myself loose. "Help!" I yelled.

Molly turned and saw me sinking. My chin hit the waves. Fido was under.

"Flap your arms," she yelled, and almost at once she rolled over the side of the boat and into the water.

I flapped, and rose some.

First off the two of us pried Fido loose, and Molly tossed her into the boat. But then the brown poodle, who didn't want to share space with Fido, jumped ship.

At least the dog could swim.

So can I, in a pool wearing my suit, but not in a flooded street towed behind a rowboat in a plastic cocoon. Molly tugged at the collapsed giraffe. I pulled. The dog circled us, barking.

Heidi kept rowing till she got to somebody's front porch, trailing us behind like a wagging tail.

At the porch I reached out, grabbed a railing, and pulled us onto the top step. Then, kicking the giraffe loose, I climbed into the boat where Toby was clutching the cat. Molly climbed in after me. R.X. reached over and scooped the poodle in. Once on board, the poodle shook, the way dogs do, and showered us all again.

When I took a deep breath, I realized I didn't smell like fish anymore. I smelled like wet dog.

"I want to go home," Toby said, whimpering.

"We are going to the Community Center," Heidi told us, as if she'd had just about enough of this, "where there are blankets and, I hope, dry clothes."

"My grandmother's going to be furious,"

Molly groaned. "When I jumped, I dropped her flashlight overboard."

"Well, it's lost forever, I'm afraid," Heidi said, and then she sighed. "I will have muscles enough to ace the Olympics by the time I get us there—*if* I get us there." The boat lurched forward.

"We'll take turns rowing," I told her, shaking my arms to get rid of the cold. "I'll take over at the corner."

"I wish we could," she said, moving us slowly on, "but if we try to shift, we'll spill."

"Oh, no," I moaned.

"Oh, yes," she told me.

"Oh, no," I said again, because what was wrong was the black bag I'd brought from the Rossis'. It wasn't on my arm anymore. "I've lost something," I said. "Something important. I think I dropped it where I sank. We've got to turn back, back to where the giraffe went down." My chill got goose bumps on it. "We have to go back."

"We can't. You know that," Heidi said.

"Besides," R.X. went on, "the water is flowing so fast that whatever you dropped isn't where you dropped it any longer."

"Was it just that garbage bag?" Molly asked.

"What was in it? Your plastic heart? That's no big deal. You can carve one out of an apple or something."

Heidi rowed slowly on. Nobody talked.

I had lost it. In the middle of the Central Street sea, the bag with the heart—and the diamonds—was gone.

5. Sugarplum and Baby Boy

Sugarplum, my little sugarplum," this huge voice wailed. Everyone in the Community Center looked up the ramp that led to the outside door. Molly's grandmother, whose vast voice fits her just right, stood at the top. Then she ran, galloping down, her arms open wide. When she got to Molly, she swept her up in a hug that swung Molly's feet from side to side like a pendulum.

Behind them my folks and Nick and his parents and a lot of other people were hurrying in, calling out names and waving. The underpass into town had been cleared, so that just before eleven o'clock in the morning the first cars were starting to get through. Now, half an hour later, the flood of relatives had reached us.

Mom gave me a big kiss, and her eyes got all bright and full of tears. "How's my baby

47

boy?" she asked, and I thought I was going to die.

"Where'd you get the terrific clothes?" Nick asked. "New style of flood pants?" I was wearing these jeans rolled up about ten times so I wouldn't trip all over them and a T-shirt, size extra-super-large, that said PARTY ANIMAL on it. Not long after we got there the night before, somebody'd brought in a stack of dry clothes, and boy, was I glad to get out of river wets.

"You spent the whole night here?" Mom asked and hugged me again. Usually we go to the center for indoor ice skating or outdoor swimming. This time we'd slept there. Heidi had been right. It was on high ground and dry.

Nick laughed at my outfit as my dad shook my hand and said, "Well, son, you're a sight for sore eyes. We sure were worried."

"I bet you weren't any more worried than we were," I told him. "Have you seen the house?"

He shook his head. "First things first."

Nick's dad just watched while Mrs. Rossi chased after Toby. I *know* the kid was glad to see his mom. He'd asked me about every four seconds when she was coming, but when she did come, instead of grabbing her knees and crying like crazy, he'd circled the room like a jet and then run into the boys' washroom.

"Are those guys over there from TV?" Nick asked me. The lights were bright on the other side of the big room near the entrance to the ice rink. Molly and her grandmother were already talking to the Channel Nine news team.

"They got here about five minutes ago," I told him.

Nick drifted off toward Molly and the lights while I told Mom and Dad and Mr. Rossi about the night before.

"Those TV weather guys should have warned us it would rain that hard," Dad said. "We'd have stayed home and saved our property, that's what we'd have done. If they can't predict a storm like that, I can't see what good they are."

"Good for nothing," Mr. Rossi agreed. "I lived here all my life," he went on, "and I never saw the river this high. I thought all those sandbags'd hold it back. For sure." Then he turned to me. "Got pretty high in the basement, did it?"

"Up to my shoe tops in the living room when I left," I told him. "And it smells."

"We'll cope," Mom said. "But both of you are alive and well, which is what matters."

"Is that Fido?" Dad asked. "The cat Molly Bosco's holding up for the TV cameras? Is that *our* cat?"

"It *is!*" Mom gave me another big hug. "You saved her, too. Oh, everything *is* going to be all right. You know, I worried about you, but I was sure you'd find a way out. You're a smart, brave boy." Hug number four.

That's me, I thought, smart and brave. The same me that was going to sail us out on a pea green picnic table.

"I was certain Fido was a gone cat," Mom went on. "It would've been my fault, too. When I left for work yesterday morning, she escaped to stalk a sparrow, and I just didn't have time to chase her down. I must thank those nice young people who picked you up. The Sheas, you said?" And she hurried off.

Mr. Rossi, who'd been wandering the floor, came back. "Got you and me some transportation," he told my dad. "Paid a kid ten bucks to let us use his boat so we can look over the damage." He shook his head. "Seems crazy. We have to rent a boat to get home in, and there's not a cloud in the sky."

"I don't much want to go," Dad told him.

"I don't either," Mr. Rossi said.

"I guess we've got to."

"I guess," Mr. Rossi said.

"We'll be back in an hour or so," Dad told me, and they headed up the ramp with a kid who was stuffing a bill in his pocket.

I waved at Nick and he made his way back to me through clumps of hugging families. I couldn't walk too well in my sagging jeans.

"Did the TV guys talk to you?" I asked him.

"No way. I missed the flood by ten miles at the dentist's office. I think they've got Molly on camera again, though. I bet she's saying how she, single-handed, kept you from drowning in the middle of Central Street. That's what she told me."

"She made that up," I told him. I couldn't let Nick think Molly had saved me. Anyway, I probably would have gotten free by myself. Maybe. "Look, it's a very long story, but basically, the boat I was in just happened to collapse. Molly didn't need to jump in like that."

"R.X. told me the boat was a plastic elephant and you and Molly looked like two drowned rats."

We had looked kind of drowned-rattish when we rolled in the night before. We could even *see* how bad we looked because by the time we got there the lights were back on. The phones, though, didn't work till morning. A lightning bolt had creamed the telephone switching station.

"It was *not* an elephant," I told him. "It was a giraffe."

"Oh, a giraffe. Well, that's different," Nick said. "Did she give you mouth-to-mouth to save you?" He was practically breaking up.

I poked him in the ribs.

He laughed harder.

I glanced at my watch. It had taken in so much water it looked like a domed swimming pool for gnats. The hands had stopped moving. "What time is it?" I asked Nick.

"Almost noon, but what I want to know is how Molly—"

"When do you think we can go home?" I asked him, knowing he didn't know.

"Stop changing the subject. Molly and R.X *both* said she dragged you up by your T-shirt."

"Look, the giraffe was surrounding me. It was pulling me under."

"Molly said she saved Fido, too."

"Well, the Fido part may be true. Fido couldn't swim very far inside that pillowcase. Boy, was she mad."

"Molly was mad?"

"Fido was mad. She'd calmed down a little by the time we got here."

"Were the TV cameras on?" Nick asked.

"I told you, they came just before you did. I think they were disappointed. We weren't starving or anything. Some guy was selling hot dogs and cheddar fries on credit at the concession stand. Toby and I split an order for breakfast. We weren't very hungry."

"I meant, were the cameras rolling when Molly rescued you." He poked me in the ribs.

I poked him back, harder.

Toby raced between us with another little kid following him. They were chasing Fido, but they'd never catch her. Both of them were shrieking. It sounded like every little kid in the place was shrieking. Little kids must *have* to shriek to make their voices grow.

The night before, the place had been pretty loud, too. We'd slept in the room where kids usually put on their ice skates for the indoor rink. All the benches are covered with carpet so the blades won't shred them. While they aren't exactly pillow soft, they weren't all that bad. Molly and I had to practically tackle Toby, though, to get him to lie down. Then, while he hugged his blanket and his damp stegosaurus, we took turns telling him Darryl Dinosaur stories. Molly told "Darryl Dinosaur Gets Sleepy." I told "Darryl Dinosaur Goes Snorkeling in the La Brea Tar Pits."

Sometimes Toby wets his pants at night. I know this for a fact. Because he was going to sleep right next to me, I made him go to the toilet right before bed. I explained to him that he shouldn't wet his pants because the real reason dinosaurs like Darryl aren't around anymore is that they wet their pants and that made them smell so bad nobody could stand being near them. They were ex-stinked.

Molly said that was a lie, dinosaurs didn't even wear pants. But Toby had had about a billion dinosaur books read to him and he knew extinct, all right. He believed me. At least he didn't wet his pants all night, even though he was sleeping in this strange place where babies were crying. And he didn't call me Scumbreath once.

"So. I guess it doesn't really matter if Molly

saved you or not," Nick said, "as long as you got here with everything."

"Right. We got here." That's all I could say. I rubbed my eyes. I'd had a really hard time sleeping, not because of the babies or the hard bench or Fido running free, but because of the diamonds. When I closed my eyes, I could see the bag bobbing in the waves, floating down the Hawk River toward the Gulf of Mexico, where it would sink to the bottom and the oysters would gobble up the diamonds to live with their pearls. I didn't know what they'd think of the heart.

"Are you OK?" Nick asked. "You aren't sick, are you? Somebody said this water could make you sick."

I just shrugged. I couldn't tell him. He's my best friend, and I couldn't tell him I'd lost his mother's brand-new diamond earrings. Nobody knew I'd lost them. I had lied to Molly and told her I'd left the earrings behind. But Nick's mother would find out soon enough. She would be mad. How could she not be? And my mom, too. I mean, after she'd said I was smart and brave. And my dad. Mr. Rossi would explode. Toby would cry. Maybe Nick would stop being my friend. It would take me a million years to pay them back. How could you cut that many lawns?

"Well, my friends," a voice behind us said, "this isn't where we usually spend Friday morning, is it?" It was the voice of someone we knew really well, our teacher, Miss Ivanovitch. I turned around. But I'd never seen her looking like *this* before. She was wearing dark green rubber boots that were more like pants than boots. They came all the way to her armpits and had suspenders to hold them up.

"What are those?" I asked, pointing at the boots. My mother would have said that was rude, but Miss Ivanovitch looked weird.

"Waders," she told us, very matter-of-fact. "Usually I wear them in trout streams, but just now I was wading through Central School. It's dreadful there. On the first floor most of the desks are cracked wide open. The books inside them are swollen huge with water. The piano in the kindergarten room is lying on its back. So much is lost."

"The water didn't get upstairs to our room, did it? I mean, our desks aren't full of river, are they?"

"No, the upstairs is dry. We'll be able to salvage most everything there. But downstairs is a different story." She shook her head.

"Can we go back to school Monday if the water's down?" Nick asked her, as if there was nothing he'd rather do.

She sighed. "Afraid not. It'll be months before we can go back to Central School. Months."

Nick and I grinned at each other. Months, she'd said. Months.

"Were there rats?" I asked, remembering R.X.'s story.

She nodded. "I saw one. They come out of sewer pipes in floods sometimes. I suppose it'll take a while to get rid of them, too."

"Rats!" Nick said. "Wow. And months before we can go to school again. Too bad."

"Too bad," I agreed, and we both grinned.

"Oh!" Miss Ivanovitch looked surprised. "I didn't say that."

"You said . . ."

"I said it would be months before we could go to *Central* School."

Molly ran up. "Great outfit, Miss Ivanovitch. It's very flattering. You should wear it more often." Molly was beaming, looking extremely pleased with herself. "Guess what I've been doing. I've just been interviewed on TV about my role in the disaster."

"Your role? You mean, like it was your fault or something?" I asked her.

"Of course not. I told the huge television audience, who are always interested in disasters, how I saved—"

"You *didn't*! You wouldn't *dare*!" If she really had told the huge television audience how I got swallowed by a plastic giraffe . . .

She smiled sweetly. "I told the television audience how I rescued your dear sweet kitty. Then I picked her up and showed her to the camera. She was reasonably happy and she purred. Everybody said that she was so cute and that I was so brave. I didn't tell them the rest." She smiled again. "I didn't want to embarrass you."

I decided to talk about something else, fast. "Miss Ivanovitch, if we're not going to school at Central," I said, to let Molly know she didn't know everything, "where *are* we going?"

"Oh!" Molly raised her eyebrows high. "Of course. We can't study in all that slime, can we."

"Why don't we just set up fifth grade here?" Nick asked. "We could ice skate for gym and have cheddar fries and Diet Dr Pepper for lunch."

"Well, I'm afraid that, cool as it may be with the ice rink, this just isn't big enough," Miss Ivanovitch explained. "Actually, while I think they've found places for everybody, all of the grades won't be at the same location. Kindergarten through third will be bused to other grade schools."

"What about us?" I asked. "Are we going to junior high?"

"Or high school," Molly suggested.

"The junior high is flooded, too. They're moving to the high school," Miss Ivanovitch said.

"Where, then?" Nick asked.

"Well, I don't know how you're going to like this. I don't even know how I'm going to like it," she went on. "While it has possibilities, I'm still not quite sure what they are."

Fido and the kids ran by again. Across the room the TV lights turned off.

"Even if everything works out, you'll have a few days off. Somebody has to take the desks and supplies out of the second-floor rooms at Central and move them to the new place. Then the teachers will take a couple more days to put things in order. Late next week, the plan is that fourth through sixth graders will start school . . . in the Wilhurst Mall."

"The Wilhurst *Mall!*" Molly shrieked. She sounded like Toby, only louder. "The one with the Black Hole video shop, open every day till midnight?"

"The one with French Fry Heaven?" Nick asked.

"One and the same," Miss Ivanovitch told us. "Only we won't go to school in the Black Hole or French Fry Heaven. We've been offered space in the old Bob's. Remember, that store in the mall that closed last summer?"

"You mean, Bob's Togs for All the Family?" I asked. This was getting weirder and weirder.

"That's it," she told us. "Robert Bobb, the man whose store it was, called the superintendent, it seems, as soon as he heard about the flood. So it was Bob Bobb to the rescue."

"Are you making this up?" Molly asked. "You're making this up, aren't you?"

"Would I do that?" Miss Ivanovitch grinned. "Actually, no, I'm not. Miss Hutter called all the teachers this morning. Apparently there was a principals' meeting quite early. I expect you'll hear about it on the news tonight, after Molly and the reasonably happy cat."

"That means we'll see you next week at Bob's?" I asked her.

"In the very best class of the mall," she said, and she headed toward the door in her long green waders, walking a little like Charlie Chaplin.

"You *are* kidding, aren't you?" I called.

She turned back to us and waved. "Social studies in the shoe department. Pass it on," she said.

6. And Here He Comes Now!

All right, people. Let's settle down."

It was our first day in Bob's Togs for All the Family. But it sure didn't look the same as when I got shorts there in the spring. All the racks and stacks of clothes were gone. So were the cash registers and the clerks and the customers and the people trying to spray you with perfume. Bob's didn't have an intercom, I guess, so Miss Hutter, our principal, was blasting us with a bullhorn. I couldn't see her, but it was Miss Hutter's voice all right, multiplied by a thousand.

"I mean settle down right now!" She was probably mad because it was already 9:30 on Thursday morning, and even though we'd lost three days of school, almost nobody was sitting down. It wasn't all our fault. Because the mall was so far away, everybody'd had to take

a school bus, and the buses were late picking us up. Then, when we finally did get to the mall, they made us come in through the store's loading dock out back.

Inside, Bob's looked a lot like an anthill somebody had poked with a stick. Kids ran around searching for where they were supposed to be. Or for where everybody else was. Or for where they used to buy sneakers. Or they ran around just to run around.

In the center of the floor were two escalators, one up and one down. Neither one was working. We'd checked it out.

I spotted Miss Hutter and her bullhorn standing halfway up the down escalator. She was peering at us over her red-rimmed half glasses.

"People! People, I know this isn't going to be easy," she said. "People, quiet down." A sixth-grade teacher was climbing the escalator to talk to her.

Talk talk talk talk. Talk echoed to the high ceilings and bounced back down again. But it was hard *not* to talk. We were going to school in a *store*. And there'd been this huge flood. Everybody had a story.

"You know what I did?" I could hear R.X.

asking some kid. "I jumped off the Lake Street bridge into the underpass right next to where this blue mini-van was sunk. And you know what I got in my mouth? A frog."

It had been some rain.

But now the sun was out. Not even a sprinkle since Friday, so the water was way down. Because of the flood, Nick's uncle had come from Chicago and taken Toby to stay with him for a few days. His uncle took Fido, too, in her Kat Karrier. Our house was such a disaster, we were afraid she'd skinny-dip in the basement sludge or escape as we carried out ripped-up carpet. Neither Toby nor Fido wanted to leave.

They were safe, though, no thanks to me. But the diamonds were still missing. Also no thanks to me. I'd sloshed back and forth across Central Street and up and down it a dozen times, looking. I still couldn't bring myself to tell the Rossis. They'd lost so much stuff. Their washer, drier, electric saw, a whole roomful of basement furniture. Our washer and drier were dead, too.

Some kids said the line the water left was practically on the ceiling of their bedrooms.

Some kids' houses weren't wet enough to complain about, so they had to make up stories.

"Did you hear," a girl was saying, "about the rats? I know this kid who saw them at school. He said the reason we can't go back there is that these hundreds and hundreds of rats and snakes are crawling in and out of desks and chewing up chalk and eating paste."

"People! Settle down!" Next to me Nick covered his ears, the bullhorn was so loud. "Now, people, I want us to pretend this school is just like Central. Let us begin our day the way we always do, with the Pledge of Allegiance."

That got everybody quiet. Our big flag hadn't made it to Bob's, so we pledged allegiance to a tiny flag Miss Ivanovitch held up. It was on a toothpick pole and looked as if it might have come from somebody's Fourth of July cupcake.

No use pretending this was like Central, though. Central had real rooms and bulletin boards and bells and lockers, and it smelled like floor wax. The store was one vast space with counters, pillars, and whole walls of mirrors. It smelled like the chocolate chunk cookies they were selling warm in a store across the hall.

"I bet for gym they let us cruise the mall," Nick said.

We weren't in the shoe department where Miss Ivanovitch had thought we'd be. Our class was in a section called Purses and Accessories near the door to the mall. We were separated from the classes beside us by chalkboards on wheels and department-store leftovers—racks with clips on them and shelves of different sizes. One of them had dusty plastic sunflowers on top and a sign that said SAY HELLO TO GOOD BUYS!

Leftover signs hung all around. Down the main aisle ceiling a shiny gold banner waved—THANK YOU FOR SHOPPING AT BOB'S. I guess not enough people said "You're welcome," or they'd still be in business. Miss Ivanovitch was a walking sign. She had on a T-shirt she'd painted herself, black with blue waves splashed across the front. Between the waves she'd written WASHED UP AT BOB'S.

Our desks were there. That much was normal. Just as Miss Ivanovitch had said, parents and other people from town and soldiers from the army base had all worked a lot of hours to bring our stuff over from Central.

A fat pink eraser arched over the chalkboard behind Miss Ivanovitch and bounced on Lisa Soloman's desk. I could hear Mr. Star yell at the kid who threw it, "That behavior is highly inappropriate." Mr. Star was our teacher in fourth, and even without a bullhorn he could yell louder than Miss Hutter.

Miss Ivanovitch hurried over and leaned around the chalkboard. "Shhhhh, Jack," she told him. "You're drowning her out."

While Miss Ivanovitch had her head turned, Lisa tossed the eraser back and then stared up at the high ceiling, innocent as a kitten. Kids on both sides laughed.

"Quiet!" Miss Ivanovitch raised her voice. "We need to hear what Miss Hutter is telling us. There's so much to remember, and voices carry especially well in this—"

"In fact, they do." It was Ms. O'Malley's voice. Her fourth-grade class was on the other side of our *other* chalkboard, and now her kids were laughing.

Meanwhile Miss Hutter kept talking, her voice sounding louder or softer as she pointed the bullhorn to one side of the escalator or the other. "Art classes," she announced, "will be held in the beauty shop on the second floor. Both gym and lunch are on two, as well."

"My mom said I could go to Burger King for lunch," Lisa whispered to Molly. "I brought money."

"So did I," Molly told her. "I'm going to have a ball in the mall this fall." Lisa giggled. Molly looked pleased with herself.

I'd brought a bag lunch, but I had a pocketful of change, too, for mall fries and for one of those cookies just out of the oven. Or maybe I'd get two—a milk chocolate chunk and a mint chocolate chip.

"One of our hard-and-fast rules," Miss Hutter went on, "is that while we are here, we will remain in our school setting. At *no* time is anyone to enter the mall. At *no* time. We will all—I must repeat, *all*—be eating in our second-floor lunchroom *every day*." Molly and Lisa gasped. "As it was at Central, a nutritious lunch with milk will be available."

Marshall looked up from the paper airplane he was folding and said, "Wait a minute. If we can't go in the mall, how is this supposed to be fun?"

Miss Ivanovitch was heading down the aisle to scoop up the plane before he could fly it when a woman in a gray jogging suit wandered kind of backwards into our class. In her hand she clutched a purple plastic bag with gold letters on it that said THANK YOU FOR SHOPPING AT BOB'S. She turned around and blinked at us as though, while she could tell we weren't for sale, it was possible we were part of some giant TV hoax.

"Pardon me," she said to Miss Ivanovitch. "I think I'm lost. Could you tell me where they've moved the towel department?" She dug around in the Bob's bag. "You see, these washcloths I bought last June have daisies on them, and I need roses to match my . . ."

"There are two hundred and seventeen of us here," Miss Hutter continued over the bullhorn, "and one of the problems is—though I'm sure we'll handle it very well—one problem is," and you could hear her sigh, ". . . is that there are only six toilets."

All 217 kids laughed.

"Your teachers will explain later how we plan to handle the washroom question."

"As soon as we know the answer," Mr. Star said behind the chalkboard, and both our classes and Ms. O'Malley's laughed again.

The shopper in the jogging suit must have thought she'd wandered into the Twilight Zone.

Nick wrote a note and gave it to Eugene behind him. "Pass it on," he said. "And remember, the magic word will be 'John.' "

While Miss Ivanovitch pointed the lost woman toward the mall door, Marshall fired off the plane, one of his finest. Zipping behind the escalators, it probably didn't crash till it got all the way to the sixth grade in Better Dresses. We heard a whoop and a laugh when it landed.

Molly poked me in the back. "I've got something for you," she whispered loud.

"Ohhhhh," Marshall said. "Molly's got something for Hobie."

"Something sweet?" Nick asked, grinning.

"Whatever it is, I don't want it," I told her.

She handed me the note Nick had written. "This isn't it, but take it anyway."

I read the note, smiled, passed it on, and started waiting for the magic word.

The bullhorn crackled. "He's coming *here*? He's coming *how*?" Miss Hutter's voice sounded really annoyed. "Oh, please ask him to come another day. Explain that we've only just gotten here and . . ." She was talking to the school secretary on the escalator steps. "He's on his *way*? He's coming *now*?

71

But I don't see how we could possibly . . ."

All talk stopped. This was worth listening to. If a kid had coughed way at the other end in Bob's Best Bargains, I think we would have heard it. Through the open door we could, for the first time, hear music playing in the mall. It was "Rudolph the Red-Nosed Reindeer." Wilhurst Mall must have run out of October music.

"I'm aware that this is something of an honor for us," Miss Hutter went on, "but it couldn't come at a more awkward time." She looked out, saw us all staring, and clicked the bullhorn off. We waited quietly. About a minute passed.

The bullhorn clicked on again. "Children," Miss Hutter said, her voice a little too cheerful, "I have a big, *big* surprise for you. We're going to have an important visitor." She cleared her throat. "Our very own state governor, Governor Marvel, is about to declare this entire county a disaster area, and he's decided to make the announcement right here. He's dropping in to see us. I mean, literally dropping in. He's already in his helicopter."

"And here he comes now," Marshall said low, sending another of his famous notebook-paper cruisers sailing high. It skimmed just under the fancy Bob's banner and past the down escalator, about two feet from Miss Hutter's nose. The whole school saw it.

"Marshall Ezry," Miss Hutter said, without even looking to see where the plane had come from, "that is enough of *that*. I'd like you to stop by my office this morning. It's in Credits and Adjustments, second floor. I think we have something to discuss."

Marshall folded his arms and sighed. He couldn't very well deny it. He was king of the clouds. But then, I guess even being famous has its problems.

Chock-ka-ta chock-ka-ta chock-ka-ta. We heard the blades whirling. "I expect *that* is Governor Marvel right now," Miss Hutter proclaimed, her voice almost drowned out by the sound.

"Or maybe it's Santa Claus," Nick said, "and Rudolph the Robot Reindeer."

Chock-ka-ta chock-ka-ta, coming closer.

"I've been informed"—Miss Hutter kept trying—"that the governor's helicopter and a press helicopter are both about to land on the far parking lot. I know you'll make them all feel welcome," she said, "and that you won't act silly. Now, this may take some time, so just go about your regular schoolwork until they arrive."

Here we were, sitting in the purse department of this store that was shaking like an earthquake, a guy we've only seen on TV was about to drop in from out of the sky, and Miss Hutter wanted us to study our spelling words. We would have rushed to the windows to look out, but there weren't any windows.

The THANK YOU FOR SHOPPING AT BOB'S sign quivered. We watched it shake. Then the tape that held one end of it snapped, and the side that said THANK YOU sagged into the main aisle. We clapped, but you couldn't hear us. The Chock-ka-tas got louder and louder until suddenly the engines cut off and there wasn't any sound at all except a little bit of "Jingle Bells" from the mall.

Marshall, who knew he was in for it anyway, had torn off a piece of notebook paper about an inch wide and a foot long. He'd split part of it in half, folded the rest under, and fastened it with a paper clip. It was your basic paper helicopter.

"Oh, Marshall," Miss Ivanovitch said as he tossed it high. We watched as the blades

74

twirled round and round and down to the floor.

Nick held up a pencil like a microphone. "As governor of your state," he announced when the paper plane landed, "I bring greetings."

And that's when it fell. The big gold Bob's sign couldn't take it any longer. It popped all its moorings and sank in a heap to the floor. Kids were laughing. Teachers were laughing. Miss Hutter put her hand on top of her head, as though it might fly off if she didn't.

Molly picked up Marshall's helicopter and held it high. "I hereby declare this school," she said, "Disaster Central."

"*John!*" Nick called out, and every kid in the room, all twenty-eight of us, raised our hands as high as Molly's was with the helicopter. "Miss Ivanovitch," Nick said, "this has been just too exciting. Can we *all* be excused to go to the toilet?"

7. Our Heroes

We were a media event. Again. Cameras flashed. Guys with mini-cams strapped to their shoulders aimed them at us.

"And you, little girl," Governor Marvel said. "What do you think about going to school in a great big department store?" Lisa was standing under the SAY HELLO TO GOOD BUYS! sign between happy Governor Marvel, who was as huge as any tackle, and red-cheeked chubby Robert "Bob" Bobb, who'd leased his place to the school board.

Lisa ran her fingers through her long shiny hair. Somebody must have told the camera people she'd won first place in the Miss Pre-Teen Personality contest, because they came first off to our room. And they picked her out right away to do the talking.

"My name is Lisa Soloman," she said, flashing her megawatt smile as if a dozen movie directors might be watching. "I think," she went on, beaming at the governor, "I think it's, like, *so* much fun here. I mean, there aren't any real walls between classes and the sound kind of bounces around and you can hear what *everybody's* saying, so none of the teachers can yell at you. We don't have a lot of our books and our regular junk here, so it's more like play school. And there's stuff like Miss Hutter saying we get to have our clarinet lessons in the freight elevator and all. I mean, it's a tragedy, like, but . . ." She took a long pause and kind of curtsied to smiling Mr. Bobb. "I'm going to have a ball in the mall this fall," she said.

Behind me I could hear Molly growl. That was *her* line.

Miss Hutter, standing next to the chalkboard, cleared her throat. "Governor Marvel," she said quietly, "perhaps you could talk with someone else. I think that's not quite the tone we want to set."

He nodded and turned away from Lisa to the rest of the class. Miss Ivanovitch had us sitting up straight in our seats. "On a positive note, boys and girls," the governor said, "perhaps you could share with us what you did to help during the disaster."

Marshall raised his hand. "I stacked sandbags along the river," he said. "Everybody in my family did. Amber was there, too." Amber Murnyak grinned.

"I saved my parrot," a kid in the back said, "and my grandmother's photo album."

"Well, we must have a list made of the brave deeds you fine young people performed," the governor told us. "Tragedies do breed heroes. And you, little boy," he said, kneeling beside me. "Did you save anything?"

Two mini-cam lights were on. If I told him I'd saved my cat, Molly would laugh. Out loud. What if I told him I'd taken a pair of diamond earrings the size of jumbo olives and then lost them? I bet there were policemen and secret service types who'd arrest me on the spot. In my head I could see those diamonds sparkle. Why hadn't Mrs. Rossi said anything? Or Nick? Maybe they'd been too busy to notice. Maybe I should just confess.

"I didn't save anything," I began. "I lost . . ." And I got a catch in my throat as if I was going to cry or something, but I wasn't. I really wasn't.

"Now, now, that's all right," the governor said, resting his hand on my shoulder. "It must be dreadful remembering the damage wrought by the flood. Was your loss great?"

Somebody snapped my picture. The cameras got closer. I felt like a criminal. Maybe I should wait to confess in the privacy of my own home. "Oh, yes, sir," I said. "It was great." Everything got quiet. In fact, I could tell him plenty about damage. "Well, for one thing," I began, "our big freezer in the basement tipped over when the water got really high, and the door on it came open and there were beef patties and raw chicken legs floating all over the place and bags of green beans and peas. And when the water went down it was really gross. You've got to hold your nose all the time the basement door is open. The junk left down there is about a foot deep and it looks like black licorice Jell-O would look if there was such a thing, and the smell is like—"

"My," the governor said. "Oh, my."

"Just go ahead and make the proclamation," a man with a clipboard told him, handing him a piece of paper. "Where do they get these kids?" the man asked the guy next to him.

Standing up very slowly, the governor smiled down on us. "We are here today at the Wilhurst Mall," he said, glancing at the words and turning away from us to face the cameras. "We are here in the heart of flood-ravaged McCarter County. We are here to declare this fine county a disaster area. It is here that people have worked together for the greater good. It is here that they have overcome hardships and here learned one of life's most important lessons. Even little children have saved the possessions of their families. They, too, should be honored. We salute you, the heroes of McCarter County."

Robert "Bob" Bobb clapped. Miss Ivanovitch clapped. Everybody in our class clapped. So did the kids in the classes on both sides of us, who couldn't even see him.

He hadn't mentioned people who lost things, just those who saved them. Toby had counted on me to save those diamonds. And I had lost them instead. That made me the opposite of a hero. That made me a villain. Like the cartoon fox.

"What was life's most important lesson?"

Marshall whispered to me. "I must have missed it."

Miss Ivanovitch leaned over his shoulder and said very quietly, "For you, Marshall, it's that one of these days you're going to make one airplane too many."

Marshall nodded and handed her a helicopter he'd just finished. In red ball-point pen he'd written *Marvel* on both paper blades.

The governor saw it, too. "Oh, my," he said. "It's a toy plane. Did you make it for me?"

"Yes, your honor," Marshall said, "just for you." Miss Ivanovitch grinned and gave it to the governor.

Marshall reached in his desk, took out a swept-back glider, and gave it to Robert "Bob" Bobb.

"I haven't seen one of these since I was a kid," the governor said. "I used to drive my teacher crazy with paper airplanes." He winked at us and then tossed the plane high. It whirled down without a sound, but the cameras began to click. He picked it up and dropped it again.

Mr. Bobb sent his glider knifing through the store sky.

The governor said Marshall was a talented

young man who had a great career ahead of him in aeronautics. Or possibly politics. Mr. Bobb agreed.

Marshall smiled at Miss Ivanovitch and at Miss Hutter, who said to him, "Later, Marshall."

"Well." The governor rubbed his hands together. "That was wonderful. Makes me feel like a kid again." Then, taking a package from the guy with the clipboard, he told us, "I didn't come empty-handed. I've brought a little something for you, too. There are, I believe, enough for everyone. These should help you in your study of our fine state. I know you've lost a lot of your learning materials."

We had. Our school library had been flooded out.

"This'll be something you'll want to take home and share with your moms and dads," he said, giving a fat stack of folded papers to Molly. "Perhaps you could pass these out, my dear."

Molly, the chosen one, smiled and began to hand them to the rest of the class.

To be really honest, they weren't what we'd always wanted. They were huge maps of the state with stars at places of historical interest and a list of the state bird, the state fish, the state insect, song, and slogan. The governor's picture was on the cover.

Even though the reporters had started packing up and heading for the mall, the governor and Mr. Bobb stopped by each class and gave out maps. Then the governor climbed halfway up the down escalator where he dropped, for the last time, the marvelous Marvel whirling helicopter, and then waved goodbye to us all.

Marshall began to crease his new map down the middle.

"Marshall," Miss Ivanovitch told him, "I think *that* would be the one airplane too many."

8. A Ball in the Wall at the Mall

T he *Chock-ka-ta*s of the helicopters had just faded into the distance when Miss Ivanovitch got our attention again. "All right, my dears," she said. "Enough for ceremony. I'll make out a seating chart tonight and assign your permanent seats tomorrow. And tomorrow morning we'll start our parts-of-the-body reports. We should have begun them Monday, you may remember. I'd like us to get back to normal as soon as possible."

Normal? We all sat blinking. What is this normal?

Beep went something near the mall door. *Beep.*

"And who was to start?" she asked. "I know the list was written on the board, but that's there and we're here and I just don't remember whose names were first."

"Tomorrow?" I asked.

"Tomorrow," she said. "Ready or not."

Beep, it went again.

"I forget," I told her.

"I don't," Molly said. "Nick's up first. Hobie's up second. I'm third. Hobie's doing the heart. Remember now, Hobie?" She and Amber looked at each other and grinned.

"Wooooo," Nick cooed. I moved my chair as far away from Molly as I could.

"Also," she went on. "Also, when do classes for the talented and gifted start up again? And do you know what we'll be doing?"

"As Miss Hutter announced earlier," Miss Ivanovitch told her, "your TAG classes will begin tomorrow afternoon at one o'clock in Infantswear, second floor. My guess is you'll talk about how people adapt to new places."

Beep.

Lisa raised her hand. "Miss Ivanovitch, I've got two things. One. I don't think it's fair we can't eat in the mall. Two. What is that beep?"

"Ah, I have three things," Miss Ivanovitch said. "One. This store is in the mall. You'll eat lunch in this store. Thus, you *will* be eating in the mall." Lisa frowned. "Two. Because of fire regulations we can't keep the door into the mall locked. What you hear is a laser beeper. They installed it this morning so we can tell when someone passes through the front door. If anyone tries to sneak out for fries and a shake, it beeps. If someone comes in to buy long winter underwear or washcloths with roses on them, it beeps. Right now they must be testing it. Three. You have changed the subject. We were talking, I think, about reports that will begin tomorrow morning."

"Oh, well, mine was on, like, the third day," Lisa said, "so I've got till at least Monday, and what I signed up to do it on is hair." She flipped hers.

"Figures," Molly said. "Lisa has the hair and Hobie had the heart." Lisa curled her lip.

I *had* the heart was right. Molly knew it was lost. I didn't know why she was being so mean about it. After school I was going to look for it and for the earrings one more time before I told someone they were lost. When the bus let me off, I'd search for the zillionth time among all the flood junk on the street.

If I didn't find the diamonds today, I'd have to start baby-sitting Toby free for the rest of my life. Maybe I could sell T-shirts that said

DISASTER CENTRAL or I SURVIVED THE FLOOD. But none of that added up to diamond money. Maybe I'd have to give up college.

If I didn't find the heart, I could just trace a picture on a piece of notebook paper or something. I could explain how the heart worked OK. I mean, I knew that stuff cold about auricles and ventricles, and arteries leading *away* and veins going *to*. But the difference between a nothing report and a great one was the missing pumping heart. Except, of course, that even before I lost it, it leaked.

"The time is eleven-twenty," Miss Ivanovitch announced, after she'd put the parts-of-the-body list together again. "And we're five minutes late for gym. Because it's our first day I'm going with you."

This was great. More exploring. Heading down the main aisle to the escalator, the first kids in line scrunched through the fallen THANK YOU FOR SHOPPING AT BOB'S banner. At every step it crackled like thin ice on the sidewalk. If somebody'd turned a hose on it, the long gold strip would have made a terrific water slide. But teachers were yelling "*Shush,*" and so Miss Ivanovitch had a couple of kids roll the dead sign up and put it on a shelf near the mall door. While they were there this one girl ran her hand past the laser light beam. *Beep.* And then again. *Beep.*

"I believe," Molly said as we started off, "that we are going to learn absolutely *nothing* at this place. A school has got to be a *real* school."

Going up an escalator that isn't working is one weird feeling. The first step is just about an inch high and the next one is only about three inches, and every time you step your foot is surprised.

Nick was about halfway up when he turned around and said, "Hey, we can spy from here!" And it was true. From where Miss Hutter and the governor had stood, you could see practically everybody. But Miss Ivanovitch wouldn't let us stop to find out who was scratching, poking, or passing notes.

When we got to the top, the first thing we noticed in our new gym were these two huge pillars with places in them for mannequins to stand. They were big enough to hide behind. It'd be a terrific place for dodge ball.

"You're my first class up here," our gym teacher, Ms. Lucid, told us. "We'll see how this works out." She started running in place. "OK, let's do a little brisk jogging to get the blood pumping." I knew how that worked. *Lub-dup.*

The gym at Central had been flooded, so I guess the shiny wood floor there was all swollen and cracked with water. This floor was carpet, brown like sand.

Shuffle, shuffle, shuffle, we jogged, sort of, past the pillars, in a big circle around our new gym. "Lift your feet," Ms. Lucid called out. "Raise those knees."

Shuffle, shuffle, faster. "Hobie," a voice behind me said softly. "It may not be fair of me to tell you this, but Molly—"

Crack! A snap of lightning hit my arm, like the one I thought would shoot through my ears in the storm. This one, though, came out of Amber Murnyak's finger. She'd touched me. I turned around. Her red curls were hopping as she ran. "What was *that* all about?" I asked her, rubbing my arm.

"Just static electricity. The rug does it. You know."

I did know.

"Lift your knees," Ms. Lucid called again, but I didn't lift them. Instead I shuffled along as if I was skating. Then I leaned forward and touched Nick on the back of his neck. He yelped.

"Static electricity," I told him. "Pass it on."

He laughed and reached out toward Molly, but her hair covered her neck, so he zapped her just above her elbow.

"Nick *Rossi!*" she yelled. "You are going to—"

"Static electricity," he told her. "Pass it on."

She laughed and then she laughed again, because in front of her was Lisa, who'd stolen her line when she talked to the governor.

Everybody behind Molly had to slow down as she pressed her feet against the rug at every step. Then she shuffled fast, pointed her finger so we could see, wiggled it a little and touched Lisa lightly on the earlobe. I could hear the crack. I half expected thunder.

Actually there was a kind of thunder. Lisa stormed. "Molly Bosco, you think you're so smart!"

"All right, girls, what's going on over there?" Ms. Lucid asked.

"Nothing," Lisa told her, but she narrowed her eyes.

Molly smiled.

"Had enough running? OK, on to the next."
Ms. Lucid was always ready to move on to
the next.

"You know what I'd like to do?" Nick whispered. "I'd really like to explore behind those
doors along the wall. I mean, downstairs they
go into old dressing rooms, and up here, who
knows?"

"First half of the line is one team," Ms. Lucid went on. "Second half starting with Michelle is another. Since the only equipment I've
got here is one kickball, that's what we'll go
for. Bob's Togs unique kickball."

We were on Michelle's team and up first.
"Slow and bumpy," Michelle called, and Eugene threw it slow and bumpy. She kicked and
a kid caught it easy.

"One out!"

"Fast and smooth," Lisa called, and Eugene
threw it fast and smooth.

THWACK, she kicked it. Lisa ice skates and
does gymnastics, and she's got major strong
legs. The ball went up and up, but nobody
caught it. Ever. It disappeared. The ceiling
swallowed it.

"Home run," somebody from our team yelled,
and Lisa ran.

"Ceiling ball. That doesn't count," a kid from the other team called, making it up.

"It's a pit ball," Molly said as Lisa's toe hit the tape that marked home plate. "Lisa made a spit pit."

"I made a home run, but I did not make a spit pit. That's disgusting," Lisa said.

At Central School, pit balls are the ones that drop into the spit pit, this gross stairwell next to the playground that's always filled with brown apple cores and test papers and crushed pop cans and wads of gum and junk like that.

"Right," Molly said.

"The spit pit is there. This is here," Lisa told her. "Besides, that hole can't be a spit pit. It's in the ceiling. You can't spit up."

"Whatever," Molly said, shrugging. "The ball is gone. Now we can't play because Lisa kicked too hard."

"Perhaps we could hum and folk dance," Miss Ivanovitch suggested. The kids all groaned.

"It's not *my* fault." Lisa was getting mad.

Ms. Lucid stared up at the ceiling hole and shook her head. "Well, at least one of the laws of nature doesn't seem to apply here. What goes up does not always come down at Bob's."

"I'll go in after it," Marshall said.

"No telling where a ladder is." Ms. Lucid sighed.

"We could build a human pyramid," Amber suggested.

"But the ball may have rolled halfway across the ceiling," Nick said. "There's got to be lots of empty space up there."

"Well, my friends, if we had a bell," Miss Ivanovitch called out, "it would be bell time. So let's just head downstairs now, then up again in half an hour for lunch in our splendid new improved Bob's Central cafeteria."

Molly rolled her eyes. Amber was digging in her jeans pocket for money.

"Amber," I said, "what was it you were going to say before you shocked me? About Molly?" This was pretty funny because Molly was standing right there.

"You wouldn't." Molly stepped back and narrowed her eyes. "Amber Murnyak, you weren't going to tell him? Are you my friend or what?"

"I just thought . . ." Amber started. "I guess," she told me, "you'll have to find out when Molly wants you to."

"Sometimes you aren't any fun, Amber,"

Molly said, and she stalked off toward the escalator.

Miss Ivanovitch turned. "Marshall," she said, "Miss Hutter sent a messenger. She wants to see you. Now."

"Hey, Nick." I was breaking up. "It looks like old Marshall is really going to get it this time. So, what do you think she'll make him do?" I turned around. "Nick?"

Ms. Lucid looked at me strangely. She and I were the only ones left in the room.

Miss Ivanovitch was heading down the escalator with the rest of the class behind her, but Nick wasn't in the line. I ran around both pillars.

"Nick," I called again. But he didn't answer.

Nick had disappeared.

9. Now You See It . . .

One, two, three soft, low whistles. I stood still, listening, trying to figure out where they came from.

"Hurry up," Eugene called back to me. "You want to get in trouble like Marshall?" Eugene was the last kid heading down the escalator.

Two short whistles, one long. I heard them again. It was the signal Nick and I had worked out to call each other when we were six years old. We've used it ever since.

"Are you waiting for someone?" Ms. Lucid asked. She glanced over her shoulder, but clearly there was no one around to wait *for*, even lurking in the far corners. The whistles didn't sound far, though. They sounded very close. Surely Nick hadn't, somehow, climbed into the ceiling spit pit. I hurried over and stared up to where Lisa's kick had knocked the tiles loose.

"Don't worry about the hole," Ms. Lucid said. "They'll be tearing the place apart and completely redoing it after we leave, anyway. We'll just have to be careful what games we play. Maybe I can borrow some stomach scooters."

Another soft whistle came from somewhere up. If I hadn't been listening for it, I wouldn't even have noticed. I looked in the direction of the sound and saw at once where it was coming from. Through a rectangular grate high on the wall in back of Ms. Lucid, something was wagging. A piece of paper. A piece of paper I had seen before. I had one just like it in my back pocket. It was the map the governor had given us. I knew for sure because I could see his picture.

Ms. Lucid turned to look where I was staring. Before her eyes got there, the paper had slipped back into the grate.

"Is something wrong?" she asked.

"Oh, no, nothing." I shook my head and swung my arms, trying to keep her looking my direction. Behind her I could see the map again. It had to be Nick on the other end because that was our whistle. "I was just thinking," I told her, "that . . . that what if I brought my kickball from home to use in gym."

97

Could Nick have crawled into a pipe? Or what? Somehow he was behind this foot-long grate near the ceiling that looked as if hot air should be blowing out of it.

"Why, that's very thoughtful of you to offer," Ms. Lucid said. "I'd be grateful if you brought it. We'll try not to make yours disappear."

While she bent to pick up a huge stack of papers, I edged toward the grate.

"You OK?" I asked. Maybe he needed saving.

But the map waved up and down like yes.

"You need help?" I asked, louder.

The map fanned back and forth like no.

"Don't need a thing." Ms. Lucid straightened up. "But it's very thoughtful of you to ask, Hobart. Good to know you're a willing worker. I expect, though, that you'd best get back to your room." She gave me a pat on the shoulder. "I do hope the flood hasn't upset you too much." She thought I'd gone bonkers.

When I looked back, the map was gone. Maybe she was right.

Sliding on the escalator handrail would have been the fastest way down. I'd have done it, too, but that would have got me back up to

Miss Hutter's office quicker than I'd got down, and she was already busy chewing out Marshall. I'd have hated to bother them. Anyway, the fourth graders were starting up both escalators on their way to lunch. So I elbowed my way down and hurried back to our room.

"Hobie, I've been looking for you," Miss Ivanovitch said as I sank into my seat. "And Nick. Do you know where he is?"

I could have just told her I didn't know, but then she might have sent out a search party. Instead I said, "He, uh . . . he had a *stop* to make. I mean, you know, he had to *go*."

"Ah, yes. Well, we're working out an orderly plan for that," Miss Ivanovitch reminded me. "After lunch I'll announce the new rules."

I didn't actually say what I meant by "stop" and "go," but then she didn't actually say what she meant by "that," either. Still, I bet she didn't mean she'd be announcing how often kids could go to the heating vents every day.

Nick had said he didn't need help. Or at least I thought that's what his map said, but map or not, if he didn't show up before lunchtime I was going to tell. Tom Sawyer got lost in a cave and nearly got killed.

I began to search the first-floor wall for more grates. On the far side I spotted one, but it didn't look suspicious.

"I can't believe I left all this in my desk," Molly was telling Amber. "I'd have been sick if the flood got it." Two by two, kids were going up to sort through a heap of brown bags piled in the front of the room. They were filled with stuff the moving people had dumped out of our desks at school before bringing the desks here. They'd emptied the contents of each desk into a separate grocery sack.

"Some of these bags have more in them," Amber said, "than the desks did."

She and Molly laughed, though it didn't sound funny to me. I guess you had to be there.

All around was the sound of kids talking, a just-before-lunch sound, a hum, like a machine running fast. Still, I thought I heard a whistle. Or two. Possibly three.

Sound carried so well in that huge space that the whistles could have come from anywhere. Could have been a kid in Mr. Star's room.

But then they came again. Three times.

From somewhere up. And I saw where from.

High on the wall above the mirrors, beyond the SAY HELLO TO GOOD BUYS! sign, something was waving out of a grate. It wasn't there long, so I couldn't tell what it was. It might have been a state map.

But Nick *couldn't* be on the first floor. I'd just seen him on the second floor.

Unless. Unless he really was crawling around through a maze of pipes. If he was, what if he turned the wrong way and got fried in the furnace or frozen in the air conditioner?

I waved at the grate. No map moved back. What if the pipe he was in had cracked? What if . . .

"You want the grocery bag with all your desk stuff?" Molly asked me. "Almost everybody's found theirs. But I think this is yours." She had two sacks on her desk, their tops neatly folded. She picked one of them up and held it out to me. "Don't you want to look inside?"

"Later," I said, waving her away. "Later. Right now I've got to decide something." Should I tell or not? If I saved Nick, I'd be Hobie H. Hero. If I ratted on him, he'd kill me.

Slowly I walked up to Miss Ivanovitch, slowly turned around to see if the map was waving again, and, since it wasn't, decided that

Nick was being swallowed by steam pipes.

Miss Ivanovitch was talking to two kids who said none of the desk stuff left was theirs.

"This is *garbage*," one of them told her, holding out a brown bag, "and not even my garbage."

"Miss Ivanovitch," I said, "I'm worried."

"Why, Hobie." She turned to me. "Is there anything I can do?"

"I think there's something you ought to know . . ." I began. First I glanced at the grate. Nothing there. Then at another grate across the room. Nothing there. "I'm afraid someone's stuck. I mean lost. I . . ."

Behind me a kid was trying to whistle "Pop Goes the Weasel." I turned and the whistling stopped. Next to the back chalkboard, heaving a little for breath but grinning as if he knew something nobody else did, was Nick.

He waved at us with his map.

"Nick, I'm glad you've returned," Miss Ivanovitch called. "There must have been quite a line. Now, Hobie, what's wrong?"

She leaned toward me. I must have looked like somebody who'd just been punched out. "Someone lost?" she asked.

"Oh, not some*one*, some*thing*," I told her,

moving toward Nick and saying the first words that came into my head. "I just thought I better tell you I lost my heart."

She blinked.

I stared at Nick to make sure he didn't disappear. "The heart I made for my report. In the flood. I lost it. I mean, I'm pretty sure I did. I . . ." Nick was laughing. "But maybe I'll find it. I'll look one more time. . . ."

"It's twelve o'clock," Molly announced.

"You're a terrific bell, Molly," Miss Ivanovitch told her. "I'm starved, too. Everybody take the escalator up to lunch. Hobie, are . . . ?"

Nick strolled over, smiling. "He's OK. Just can't handle school in a store."

Maybe I'd imagined his being up near the ceiling. Probably he was in the john all that time. "Nick," I said, "where have you—"

"And, of course," he went on, "Molly gets him all flustered. He thinks she's really cute."

Molly laughed as if she knew it was true, and she and Amber headed off, whispering, for lunch.

"I do not!" I said, loud enough for Molly to hear, and I grabbed the grocery bag with my junk in it off her desk and shoved it under my chair.

"It's OK," Nick told Miss Ivanovitch brightly. "Nothing a little peanut butter and jelly won't fix. I'll feed him." He clamped his hand on my elbow and steered me toward the escalator.

As we walked down the big main aisle, he apologized. "Look, I'm sorry I said that about Molly, but I had to keep you from asking about the mystery." Then he lowered his voice. "After lunch, when no one is looking, I'll show you what I've discovered. It's this amazing place." And then he snapped my nose with the map.

10. I Spy

Can you believe this place?" Nick asked. "How long do you think we can keep it a secret?"

"I bet they make it off limits," I told him.

"I bet it already is," he said.

We were peering down from behind a metal grate high above the first floor of Bob's Togs for All the Family. It was the grate where, from our class, I'd watched the map wiggle. Through the slots we could see what practically everybody was doing, this side of the escalator. The view was spectacular.

"Look down by the second chalkboard," I said, pointing. "Over there. Mr. Star is talking to Miss Ivanovitch. What do you think they're saying? You think they're wondering where we are?"

Even if they'd seen us watching them, they'd never have guessed exactly where we were.

They'd have thought we were wedged in a heating pipe, hot air shooting out around us. Actually we were in a stockroom, standing on this wooden platform about six feet off the floor.

"They aren't talking about us," Nick said, as if I was some kind of nut. "First off, it's not bell time yet, and second, I bet they're talking gooey to each other."

"I bet they aren't," I told him.

"You never can tell," he said.

Far across the huge room kids were streaming through the door from the loading dock and then clumping up in their class spaces. From high above we could watch them all.

"I bet store detectives stood up here," Nick said, "so they could see who it was if some gang came in and stole . . ."

"Diamond earrings." It was all I could think of.

"Yeah, diamond earrings. They'd catch those guys and smash them. Hey, look, that kid's trying to crawl under the laser beam. Ms. O'Malley's going to cream him. Ha. But we saw him first. This is great."

It felt like a tree house. A black velvet curtain hung behind us, blocking the light, so we could see out but they couldn't see in. The place was *built* to spy from.

And that's what we were doing—spying. For a while we watched kids in the long line to the washrooms zap each other with electric sparks.

"Hey, catch Marshall. In our room," Nick whispered. "That guy's got to be crazy. He's making another airplane. Out of some kind of shiny paper."

"Miss Ivanovitch isn't paying any attention. She and Mr. Star are walking away," I said. "If they caught him, they'd make him stay after school till Thanksgiving."

"You know, Marshall wasn't outside at lunchtime," Nick told me. "I figure he was up in Miss Hutter's office crying for mercy or something."

After lunch they'd sent us all out to run on the big asphalt parking lot in back. The whole area was blocked off, and people who'd planned to use the lot stopped their cars and scratched their heads, wondering who we thought we were, anyway.

Nick and I had hung out on the old loading dock, the official school entrance. When they let kids back in, we were the first. Then, Nick leading the way, we'd kind of fast-walked past our class and into the stockroom where the ladder to the spying place was.

"You think anybody saw us sneak in?" I asked him.

"If they did, they'd have followed us," he said. "But we gotta be careful when we leave."

"Wait a minute. You never told me. How'd you get down here from that second-floor vent upstairs?"

"Magic," he said. "When I closed my eyes and repeated the secret words, 'Open, Bob's Togs,' the floor split open to reveal this dark cave. I fought my way down past three huge, drooling mastiff dogs and suddenly found myself here. Magic, plain and simple."

"Cute," I told him. "Then you can just magic us back up. I want to see if they've fixed the spit pit."

His grin was wicked.

"OK, how'd you *really* do it?"

He laughed out loud and a kid below us looked in our direction, so we pulled away from the vent and shut up for a second. Then he whispered, as if he was letting me in on some super state secret, "The back stairs are right around that corner."

I leaned my head against the fake vent and sighed. Some magic. He'd walked down.

"Look, I think Amber likes R.X. They're talking," he said, pointing.

I didn't see them, but I did see Lisa getting ready to do something she shouldn't. You could tell. She was standing next to Molly's desk, glancing around to make sure nobody was watching.

I watched. She grabbed the big brown bag that was on top of Molly's desk and quick stuffed it into the wastebasket next to Miss Ivanovitch's desk. Then she strolled over, picked up one of the bags that nobody had claimed, and plopped it down where Molly's bag had been. Miss Ivanovitch was nowhere in sight. I was the only one who saw.

One brown bag looks pretty much like another. Might take Molly a while to find out her sack was gone. Unless. Unless it was found by me, Hobie H. Hero.

"It's almost bell time. We better get back while we can," Nick said. "I could stay up here all afternoon."

"I'll sneak out first," I told him, "like the invisible man." The light was dim so I took it slow. Easing my way to the floor, step by step,

I leaned forward, glancing through the rungs of the ladder. Something was lying in the dark shadows under the platform, something that looked like . . . an arm. And farther back, near the corner, the outline of . . . Bending closer, I blinked my eyes, and looked again, and yelped. I almost screamed bloody murder.

"Quiet," Nick hissed.

I couldn't help it, though. This was scream stuff. I took a deep breath, stepped off the ladder, and then took another. My knees bent like gummy worms. "Nick," I whispered, "get down here fast." I closed my eyes. "There's an arm, and maybe there's a head in the corner. And I think it's got long black hair like Miss Ivanovitch has." I looked into the dark again. "A lot like Miss Ivanovitch. I didn't see her out there, did you?"

Nick leaped down and looked where I was looking. The hair was all messed up, and you couldn't make out the face except for lots of red on the mouth, and eyes that were open wide. It was gruesome.

"What are we going to do?" I was breathing hard.

Nick pushed in front of me, moved in toward the corner, and bent down over the head. Then his shoulders began to shake. I almost ran.

"What we're going to do," he said, soft and scary quiet, "is shake a leg. Right now." Then he wheeled around and I saw that he'd grabbed the hair, all that wild black hair. "And we're going to take *this* with us." He stuck it in my face.

I felt as though my own head was going to spin right off. The long black hair that Nick was waving at me didn't have anything under it. The head still lay in the corner.

But it took me about three gulps of air to see that the hair he was waving was not a scalp but a wig, and the head and the arm under the steps were just parts of a broken manne-quin that Bob's had left behind. I thought Nick was going to die. Laughing.

Sitting down on the bottom step, I laughed, too. "Any loose legs in the corner for us to shake?" I asked him.

"All right, people." Inside the store Miss Hutter was back on the bullhorn.

I got up. "We're going to get in deep trouble. Toss the hair back where it came from and let's get out of here."

"Back where it came from?" He hurried over and picked up the head by the neck. "You've got to be kidding. Just look at this." He held it at arm's length. The head was the color of skim milk, except for the gray where its chin was slightly chipped. Half of one ear was gone and the nose was cracked. The big brown eyes had lots of lashes painted around them. The red mouth looked sad. "If we left it here it might cry," he said.

"But if we take it to class, we'll have to tell where we got it, and they'll discover our spy place."

He shrugged. "They'll discover it, anyway. By Monday, tops, there won't be any secret places left, and it'll be just like regular school. Still, we'll leave the arm for tomorrow. If we left the head, somebody else might find it and use it to scare innocent children."

He tickled the back of my neck with the wig. I stomped on his toe.

Waiting a second in the stockroom doorway, we watched a bunch of teachers, Miss Ivanovitch among them, walking down the escalator steps.

"So, what are you going to do with that thing?" I asked Nick. "They won't let you keep it."

"I'm thinking," he said. "I'm thinking."

"You might say it's part of an act you're getting together, a ventriloquist act," I told him.

"You mean I could hold the head on my knee and make it sing stuff like, 'I Ain't Got Nobody'?"

"Actually, I was thinking about *you* as the dummy. She can throw her voice without moving her lips a whole lot easier than you can."

"Do you mind," he said, handing me the wig, "if we break out into the real world?"

Instead of crawling on our bellies or walking backward, we just strolled onto the main floor, head and hair in hand, and nobody seemed to notice. At Bob's Togs, weird things were normal.

We were passing between two classes separated by chalkboards and sweater racks when the bullhorn clicked on again.

"People," Miss Hutter's voice announced. "People, may I have your attention please. I have something important to say."

The place got instantly, amazingly quiet. I mean, maybe this time she'd announce the president was coming to hand out hero medals.

"Thank you." You could hear her sigh. "I do

believe you're my good, polite, well-behaved Central School students again." Nick and I stood still, good, polite, and well-behaved, a brown-eyed head and a mass of black hair tucked under our arms. "I told you this morning," she went on, "that while we were here, no one would be allowed to enter the shopping mall. Usually that will be the case. At this time, however, I must announce an exception to that rule."

11. Larry Lion, Talking Trash Can

*O**o-gah oo-gah!* We didn't know whether to move or not, so Nick and I froze at the back of our class as Miss Hutter, high on the escalator, blared out this screaming *oo-gah* siren.

"Remember that sound, people," she said. "Whenever you hear it, that means we are having a fire drill. At that time—*and at that time only*—classes near the mall door will break the no-mall rule. At fire drill time they will, at their teachers' direction, file through the laser beeper straight into the center of the mall." That was us.

"Yeah!" We clapped and stomped our feet.

"Children in classes near our main loading-dock door will, of course, *not* enter the mall, but will exit directly into the parking lot."

"Boo." Those kids moaned.

"People!" Miss Hutter warned. "And during

the drill, you will, as always, observe the rule of silence." The silence rule we knew. When we were in kindergarten, we'd lock our lips up tight before fire drills and throw the keys away. If there was also a rule about not buying onion rings and cookies during a drill, Miss Hutter didn't mention it.

As soon as the bullhorn clicked off, Miss Ivanovitch called Nick and me to the front of the class. She pointed at a spot on her desk, where Nick carefully placed the head. I held the black hair high and dropped it on top. It slithered down, covering one big brown eye and half the cracked nose.

"And just how do you explain this?" Miss Ivanovitch asked, looking grim, as if the wrong answer might get us three weeks after school.

"I think the wig must be at least one size too big for the head," Nick told her. "Which would explain it." She did not smile. That was not the right answer.

"Miss Ivanovitch," I tried, "we thought you would want us to get a*head* in class."

She groaned, then crossed her arms and waited.

"This is . . ." Nick started, rolling the thought around like a marble. "This is Sylvia.

Sylvia here has kindly agreed to help me give my parts-of-the-body report. Haven't you, Sylvia?"

Slowly the wig, like some huge hairy spider, began to crawl off the head. It slid onto the desk, slipped to the edge, and dropped on the floor upside down.

Miss Ivanovitch raised one eyebrow.

"I'm up first thing tomorrow," Nick said fast, "but I've brought her in a day early to get acquainted. She's kind of cut off from the world."

Miss Ivanovitch looked closely at the head and the scrambled hair on the floor. "Your report is on . . . baldness?" she asked.

"Oh, no," he told her. "Sylvia's going to show us her salivary glands."

"Salivary glands?" She turned the head around to face her.

"They're in there," he explained, facing it frontward again and tapping the neck. "Excuse me for pointing, Sylvia," he whispered in the good ear. "They make spit," he told the class. "Two cups a day."

The kids were breaking up. So, in fact, was Miss Ivanovitch.

"Syl and I are also doing this incredible experiment," he went on, "with starch and sa-

118

liva. I don't see how I could possibly go on without her." Then he bowed, swept the wig up from the floor, and tucked it under his arm, and we both sat down.

The class was quiet, waiting to see what Miss Ivanovitch would do.

She picked up the head, cocked it to the side, then handed it over to Nick. "Better put her hair back on," she said. "I wouldn't want her to catch a head cold."

I think Sylvia almost smiled. Nick had saved both her and us. Our hero.

"But now," Miss Ivanovitch went on, "let me tell you all—except, of course, Sylvia—about washroom passes."

She held up a little yellow square with a smiley face stamped on it. "This is a washroom pass. I will give you each one every morning. As Miss Hutter explained, there's a toilet shortage here. Naturally you can use the washroom before school, after school, and at lunchtime, but unless you have a real emergency, we're limiting you to one absence from class a day to go the toilet. Not that we thought you'd actually cheat or anything, but you do see a number of teachers every day—in gym, art, music, and special classes—so we decided that the best way to keep the toilet line down was to hand out passes, starting tomorrow."

"There were about twenty people in line when the bell rang," some kid said.

"If the line's too long, come back and try later. At the end of the day I will collect all unused passes. OK?"

Marshall had spent almost the whole lunch hour making bathroom passes. That was his punishment. He'd been at the paper cutter slicing out hundreds of squares from yellow construction paper and stamping them with faces. Now all the teachers had a supply.

"They're exactly one and five-eighths inches square," Marshall explained, as proud as if they'd been planes. "*Very* carefully done and almost impossible to copy."

Marshall's face was strangely smug, as though he'd just eaten a nutty fudge bar that somebody'd told him he couldn't have. He lifted the corner of a sheet of paper on his desk so I could see a whole mess of grinning passes, maybe twenty of them, made by hand by Marshall—and kept.

I smiled at him. Maybe he would share. He was my friend.

"By the way," Miss Ivanovitch went on, "you can't imagine what is going to happen to Marshall."

I knew it. Something worse had to happen than making those paper passes he could sell or trade for bubble gum.

Nick raised his hand. "Hobie thinks Miss Hutter gave him a month of after-schools. I think she said if he shoots one more plane he can't touch paper again till sixth grade."

We all turned to see if Marshall was crying or at least making weird faces. Instead he looked like someone who'd just swallowed another richer, nuttier piece of forbidden fudge.

Miss Ivanovitch laughed. "Nick, if I were you and Hobie, I think I'd be very cautious about suggesting punishments."

I slid down in my seat.

"What is going to happen," she went on, "is actually rather nice. We all know that Marshall makes amazing paper airplanes, some of which he *used* to throw when he shouldn't. But that was before he reformed. Right, Marshall?"

Marshall nodded gravely.

"Well, when the governor came, he thought Marshall's airplanes were terrific. He thought

Marshall was terrific, and he has asked Marshall to represent the youth of the state at the opening of the new west suburban airport this Saturday."

Marshall grinned hugely, not even trying to look humble.

"For the airport dedication," Miss Ivanovitch went on, "he has been asked to launch the very first plane—one of his own design. Marshall has, I think, agreed."

He nodded, reached into his desk, and pulled out the sleek shiny flier Nick and I had watched him fold when we were in the spy place.

It seemed to me that now they were making *Marshall* into some kind of hero.

"Is that fair?" Eugene asked, raising his hand. "I mean, he wasn't even supposed to throw those planes. It's *not* fair."

"As you all know, Marshall is extremely able and . . . high-spirited. I think he represents this class pretty well, don't you, Sylvia?" she asked the head on Nick's desk. Sylvia nodded yes. Her hair slipped forward.

"But now it's time to talk of numbers," Miss Ivanovitch went on. "Can anyone besides our balding friend here tell me how many feet the Hawk River rose last week? And, even more puzzling, why? Why were we caught by surprise when—"

Oo-gah oo-gah oo-gah! I took a deep breath. No smoke smell. Fire drill. I guess Miss Hutter must have figured this was a lost day anyway and we might as well get the first drill under our belts.

Miss Ivanovitch, letting her questions go unanswered, put her finger to her lips. Nobody spoke. When the *oo-gah*s died down, except for the scraping of chairs the whole first floor of Bob's was silent.

As we began to file out, Lisa glanced around to see if anyone was watching her, just the way I'd seen her do when I was in the spy place. She hung back and made a detour to Miss Ivanovitch's wastebasket. I stepped behind her and watched as she lifted out the brown sack I'd seen her sneak off Molly's desk. She swung it at her side as she walked.

I moved into line behind her.

Beepbeepbeepbeep. Every time a kid went through the laser beam, it beeped. I set it off going forward, backed up a step, and found out it worked that way, too. Then I beeped it again going into the mall. It wasn't exactly silence, but my lips were sealed.

When I stepped from school into the mall, the world didn't turn from black-and-white to Technicolor. It wasn't Oz or Disney World, just the mall. Basically, things hadn't changed that much since the last time I'd been there, buying socks with my mom a couple of weeks before.

A woman pushing two babies in a stroller stopped to stare at the flow of kids pouring out of Bob's Togs for All the Family. "What's going on in there?" she asked Lisa, but Lisa just smiled.

Nobody said a thing. We stared back at the woman, obeying the rule of silence. The guy behind me put his thumbs in his ears and waggled his fingers at the little kids. Making a fast right turn, the lady aimed the stroller toward the door, and, without looking back, made her exit. Fast.

Those food shops have huge fans that shoot smells of the stuff they're cooking out into the mall. They must have set the fans on high, because as we walked past we were almost blown over by waves of chocolate chunks and

124

chicken bits and tacos and baked potatoes and pizza with pepperoni.

At the end of the fast-food lanes, just outside French Fry Heaven, there sat a big, brand-new orange trash can that looked like a lion ready to spring. Its green eyes shifted back and forth, searching the mall forest for litter-bugs.

"Hello there," it said, from a speaker in its belly. "I'm Larry Lion, Talking Trash Can. Feed me."

As kids passed, they stared at Larry, their mouths shut. One guy threw a piece of paper through the fangs. It looked like a map of the state.

"Yummy," Larry said.

Another kid tossed in a wad of green bubble gum.

"Scrumptious," the trash can roared.

Lisa, in front of me, took a little skip, reached out, and heaved the brown grocery bag down the lion's throat.

"I'm proud of you," Larry purred in his friendliest lion voice.

Lisa saw me watching her and grinned, as if we shared a secret she knew I wouldn't tell.

But she'd thrown away the very sack I'd

planned to rescue so Molly would say, "Oh, Hobie, you've *found* all my treasures." Now that idea was down Larry Lion's gullet.

The line stopped. Bob's must have emptied out fast. Miss Ivanovitch stationed herself across from me, watching for talkers. We stood and we stood. A fireman walked past, checking. We stood some more.

Down the mall you could hear the rumble of a little lift truck and see its yellow light flashing as it picked up trash cans and dumped the junk inside. Maybe Molly wouldn't miss the stuff in her bag too much. Maybe she wouldn't have cared even if I had saved it.

Still, when she found out it was gone, she would stomp her feet like Rumplestiltskin and demand to know who had taken it. Lisa smiled at me again, as though we were in this together.

Ooo-gah oo-gah. The blast came from inside Bob's. The non-fire was out, and the line was beginning to move past the smells once again.

Behind me Larry Lion growled softly.

12. Gulp

olly and Amber were waiting at my desk. Molly wasn't frothing yet or huffing-and-puffing mad.

"Did you open it?" she asked, pointing to my brown bag.

I shook my head.

"Go ahead, open it," Amber told me.

"Why don't you open yours first?" I asked Molly. It was *her* face I wanted to see. She was the one who had a fake sack, with all her real stuff dropped down a lion's throat on top of a wad of green bubble gum. Lisa stood a row away pretending to comb her hair. She winked at me.

They were waiting for me to open my sack. They wanted me to open my sack. They must have put a plastic tarantula inside, I decided, or maybe even a real frog. The flood had brought out lots of frogs.

"Open it!" Molly said again.

Kids were starting to stare, so I thought, why not? The worst thing that could happen was if it had been filled with dead river rats, only one of them wasn't. So I pulled out the bag, turned it upside down, and watched stuff pour out onto my desk.

There weren't any rats, but I sure smelled one.

On top of the heap of junk was a stack of math papers. I didn't save my math papers. Besides, these had A's on them, which made them automatically not mine. Underneath them was a half-empty package of rainbow stickers, two fuzzy blue pencils, a bunch of paperback books with girls on the covers, and some little note cards decorated with unicorns.

"This isn't my bag," I told Molly patiently, figuring I'd be nice about it. "OK, what's going on? You can tell Uncle Hobie."

"Oh, all that's *mine*," Molly said, glancing at the pile-up. "You must have taken the wrong one." She scooped up her stickers, cards, papers, books, pencils, and a stray Snoopy eraser. "*This* one's yours then." Picking up the sack from her desk, she held it behind her. "But you've got to guess what's inside."

Miss Ivanovitch was coming. I tried to grab the bag from Molly.

"Guess," she said.

"I don't know. I don't remember. Old paper stars. Magic Markers. Now & Later candy. I don't know. This is a dumb game." I grabbed again.

"It's something *I* put in today. It's something I found and brought to school. Something you want," she said. "I've been trying to give it to you all day, practically, but you wouldn't pay any attention."

"Give it to me now," I said, mad.

"OK." And she threw the sack with both arms. "You aren't any fun. I wanted you to be surprised. Yesterday walking down Central Street I saw this black bag stuck in the bottom branches of a bush, and I was almost sure it was that dumb bag you lost when you sank in the giraffe. I took the trouble to slosh across the grass to look. Even though the bag was all filled with yuck, I could see there was a plastic heart model inside. . . ."

I hugged the sack she'd thrown at me. Could she have found it? Could she have really found it?

"And so I brought it to you," Molly went on. "What do you say?"

"Anything else in the bag?" I asked her.

"I didn't look," she said. "It was too disgusting. Aren't you going to thank me?"

The diamonds were still there. They had to be. I sank down in my seat, opened the sack, and looked in. The black bag wasn't on top. I stuck my hand down deep, not wanting to empty the sack in front of everybody. The first thing I grabbed, though, was a note. The name on the front was Tiffany, and Tiffany wasn't even in school today. I reached in again and brought out a long gray dog that had *Happy Birthday, Tiffany* written on it and girls' names signed in red and green ink.

"There's nothing to say thank you for," I told Molly. "The heart's not here. Some joke. This isn't even my sack." I poured the stuff out. My desk was a landslide of paper. But no black bag. No black bag with a little box of big diamonds inside. "OK, where is it?"

She shrugged.

Miss Ivanovitch was settling down at her desk. "I can't find my sack," I told her. "This isn't mine, and Molly says my lost heart was in mine."

Amber and Molly started to giggle. Miss Ivanovitch must have thought the whole thing was some boy-girl stuff because she shook her head and said, "Hobie, I'm beginning to wonder whom you've lost your heart *to*. You've been acting *very* strangely on a day that is strange enough already."

"Oh, no," Lisa moaned. She'd been standing nearby all the time pretending not to watch, but now she was staring, her mouth open. "Oh, no," she said again.

And suddenly, just like that, I knew what she meant by "Oh, no."

I knew where my bag was. I knew where my heart was, and the diamonds. I had taken Molly's bag by mistake. So that meant it was *my* bag I'd seen Lisa exchange. It was *my* bag she'd tossed in the trash can.

The diamonds were in the garbage. They were sunk in Larry's stomach with leftover fries soaked in ketchup. At least I hoped they were. The little forklift truck had been moving down the mall, its yellow light flashing. What if it was already there and they were just about to pull off the lion's head and dump the diamonds in with half-eaten hot dogs, all set to take them off to Mount Trashmore?

131

I had to do something fast. First I looked for Nick. He was at his seat, drawing salivary glands on Sylvia with a green Magic Marker. Anyway, it would take too long to explain.

Reaching under the paper on Marshall's desk, I grabbed two smiley-face bathroom passes, handed them to Miss Ivanovitch, said, "This is an emergency," and hurried out as though if I didn't, I would explode.

"No one is to enter the mall," Miss Hutter had said. "A hard-and-fast rule," she had said. I didn't run. I didn't want anyone to stop me. I just walked fast, and when I got to the mall door, I crawled under the laser beeper that beamed about two feet off the ground.

A sixth grader saw me. "Hey!" he yelled, and I waved back as if this was an excursion somebody had OK'd.

Then I ran. When I got to the lion, it was telling this little kid that the chocolate ice cream cone he'd tossed in was "Grrrr-and."

Not far under that ice cream had to be the sack I was looking for.

The little kid's littler brother was about to pitch in a huge cup of orange stuff he'd had about two gulps of.

A few yards down the mall, the yellow light

was flashing next to Bernie Bear, Talking Trash Can, whose head was already off.

"Excuse me," I said to the kid, pushing in front of him. "The lion ate something I need. Besides, you'll probably get very thirsty later and wish you still had that."

"Keep the mall tidy," Larry growled.

I figured if I had to, I could crawl inside. Larry was a very big lion. But what if he bit? What if he was a trash compactor in disguise and smashed his food before he swallowed it? I stuck my hand in his mouth. Nothing happened, so I stuck my head in.

"Thanks a bunch," Larry told me. His voice echoed loud on the inside. Forcing my shoulders and arms in, I pushed forward. His innards were dark and smelled like your basic backyard garbage can.

"Scrumptious," he roared, and what tasted good was *me.*

I began to scoop down with both hands, feeling all over for a brown grocery sack with a black plastic bag inside, but I couldn't see colors, and the lion's belly seemed to be filled with soggy paper and wet plastic.

"Can I help?" this voice behind me asked. "I mean I'm, like, really sorry." My hands were

133

empty. I pulled out my head and turned around. Lisa was standing there looking as though she'd just made the last out in the championship kickball game.

"Really, truly sorry," she said. "It's just, Molly thinks she's so smart. I just thought it would be, like, funny to toss her dumb sack. I mean, it was on *her* desk. I didn't know the stuff was yours."

"Forget it," I told her, "and, yes, you can help. Hold my feet so I don't make a meal for this guy." Taking a huge breath, I dived into the lion's jaws again.

Lisa grabbed my legs to keep me from hitting bottom. This time I scooped straight down and came out holding a sack. Brown.

It looked right. But when I stuck my hand inside, I pulled out a mess of fish sticks and tartar sauce. I threw it back, and always polite Larry said, "Thank you."

People were staring at us.

"We lost something terribly important," Lisa told them, smiling sweetly. She didn't know *how* important.

Once more I hitched myself up to the open jaws, and once more I dived in, Lisa holding my ankles. I grabbed a sack. When I pulled it

out, it looked right, too. To keep people from asking us questions, we moved around to the lion's tail and sat on the marble floor.

"Cross your fingers," I told Lisa.

The trash truck rolled up and a guy hopped off.

"What's so important, anyway?" Lisa asked. "A bunch of old dittos and some ball-point pens? Whatever it is, we better, like, get back, or they'll kill us. Nobody knows we're out here, you know. I vaulted the beeper, so nobody heard me leave."

The trash guy lifted the head off Larry.

Inside the sack, right on top, was a red ruler with *H.H.* scratched on it. And under that—I closed my eyes, pulled out a plastic bag, crossed my fingers, opened my eyes a crack, and looked. Next to me the lion was hanging, feet up, over the trash truck, dumping everything he'd had for lunch.

I yelped. It was *the* bag. It was the one I'd filled on the day of the flood, muddy but untorn. The heart model was whole. No truck had run over it. All the red stuff had drained out, of course, but I could fix that.

I couldn't see the black velvet box, but my fingers found it. Still soaking wet, it filled my hand. Without taking the box out of the sack, I flipped its top open with my thumb. The earrings inside were cool to touch, and they felt as big as robins' eggs.

I smiled at Lisa. I wasn't mad at her anymore. Even though she didn't know it, she'd watched me rescue the diamonds. I'd saved them. I'd stuck my head in a lion's jaws and become a genuine Hobie H. Hero.

"You know what?" Lisa asked. "You've got tartar sauce in your hair."

The man sat Larry Lion's huge maned head back on his shoulders.

"Thank you," he roared, "for keeping the mall tidy."

13. Finished

Brave?" Molly asked as we piled on the bus for home. *"Brave?"* she asked again, as if I'd just used some four-letter word. "How can you say Lisa was *brave?* She stole the sack!"

"I didn't say she was brave to take it. I just said she was brave to *say* she'd taken it. I wouldn't have told on her. I was going to say I'd found it in the boys' washroom."

"I think," Molly said, "she just wanted everybody to know she'd held your hand."

"My feet," I told her.

"Same difference."

Nick slid into the seat next to me. He'd zipped Sylvia inside his jacket so kids couldn't play catch with her. He was taking her home, wigless, to perfect his salivary gland drawings, though to me she just looked as if she'd been tattooed with bunches of green grapes.

As we rolled toward Marshall's stop, he leaned over our seat. "You really blew it for me, Hanson," he said. "Miss Ivanovitch had to know where those washroom passes you used came from, and the only source she could think of was me."

"Sorry," I told him. "Did you give her the rest?"

He grinned. "Not all. I figure I can still get time out of gym, art, TAG, and spelling for the next two weeks. Still, I've got a feeling tomorrow is going to be a whole lot stricter than today. You really got away with murder, you know that?"

"*I* did? What about Nick and the head? And you? They practically crowned you king for shooting airplanes."

"Come on, you got away with a lot more than I did," he said. "It was either because today was the first day at Bob's or because Miss Ivanovitch was in a very good mood."

Nick scooted away from me toward the aisle. "She didn't keep him after school because she couldn't stand the garbage smell. 'What has two legs, a plastic heart, and flies?' " he asked.

"Hobie Hanson," Marshall answered, holding his nose. The bus ground to a stop. "See you guys tomorrow," he said. But before he left, he secretly handed each of us one grinning yellow washroom pass.

Molly moved over to Marshall's seat behind us. "You think you can get that heart pumping by tomorrow morning?" she asked me.

"Sure," I told her. "I'll just glue the seams and fill it up with cranberry-grape juice."

"You know what I'm using for my model?" she asked.

"I'll bite," Nick told her.

"I bet you don't," she said. "I'm bringing a real, live brain."

Lisa leaned across the aisle. "You are not."

"I'm not talking to you anymore," Molly told her. "Well, not a real, *live* brain, but a real one, anyway."

"Where are you getting a real brain?" Nick asked. The bus stopped for her to get off.

"My grandmother got one for me and froze it." She stood up and headed for the door. "It's a calf's brain. People eat them."

"Sick," Lisa said.

Mrs. Rossi was waiting for Nick and me as we climbed off the bus at our corner. She was holding Fido. Toby was with her, just back from Chicago. He was wearing red rubber boots because the ground was still mushy. Darryl was tucked under his arm.

"We ate out all the time at Uncle Scott's," Toby told us, "because he doesn't cook anything but cornflakes. He let me eat shark with lots of ketchup. It was very good. Darryl ate out, too. Fido stayed home."

We sat down on the Rossis' front steps and told Mrs. Rossi and Toby about school at Bob's, and the governor, and the hole in the gym ceiling, and the head in the dark corner. Toby liked the part about the helicopters best.

We would have told them more, too, but Nick spotted Molly coming way down the block. By a rope at its throat, she was pulling her inflatable sinking giraffe. She must have patched the holes, because its long neck stretched up high.

Nick rolled his eyes. "Listen," he said, "I hate to bail out like this, but I've got a lot of work to do on my report for tomorrow. It ought to be *very* good. Two heads are better than one,

I always say." He walked slowly up the steps and into the house, balancing Sylvia's head on top of his.

Fido jumped off my lap, so I got up and walked across two lawns to meet Molly and the giraffe.

"Hey, thank you for finding the bag," I told her. "I mean, I'm sorry I didn't say it before. I was really scared when it wasn't in the grocery sack I thought was mine."

She shrugged. "That's OK."

"I guess I should show you what was in it." I stuck my hand in my pocket, pulled out the wet black velvet box, and put it in her hand.

"You're kidding." She sucked in her breath. "I don't believe it. You're kidding." And she was just about to snap the box open to check that I wasn't kidding when Toby came running up, and I grabbed it back before he could see.

"Is this for me?" he asked Molly, throwing his arms around the giraffe's neck.

"It is if you'll feed it," she told him.

"Does it eat shark?" he asked.

"Shark and gummy worms," she said. He nodded and grabbed the rope.

When we got to the Rossis', Toby circled the

giraffe, inspecting it and poking it with his fist like a punching bag.

He said thank you to Molly about a million times, and then Mrs. Rossi, Molly, and I sat on the steps and watched him play on the sidewalk.

"Mrs. Rossi," I said, after there'd been this long pause, "I've got something to tell you." I didn't know how to say it and I didn't want to, but I figured she had to find out sooner or later.

I reached in my pocket, pulled out the box, and gave it to her. "Toby was worried about these during the flood," I said. "So I took them with me."

"Oh," Mrs. Rossi gasped. "I'd been wondering why they weren't on my dresser. We'd been so busy that . . . Well, they were new and I couldn't remember where I'd put them." She flipped open the box, took one fat diamond out, and held it up so it caught the light. It was the kind of earring a queen ought to wear. "And you've had them all this time."

"Well, not *all* this time," I began.

"You know, I was rather hoping they were lost," she said.

Molly and I looked at each other. "So you

could collect the insurance?" Molly asked.

"Insurance?" Mrs. Rossi looked puzzled.

"You have insurance, of course," Molly said, "in case you get robbed or they fall out of a boat and drop into . . ."

"Into a flooded street or something," I added.

"This box, in fact, feels a little as though it had spent some time in a flooded street . . . or something." Mrs. Rossi squeezed the box, and water dripped on her jacket.

"Well, after Toby gave them to me to save," I explained, "Molly's giraffe sprung a leak and I sank, and the earrings sank, too, only they didn't come to the top again when I did. Molly found them yesterday stuck in a bush."

"But then Lisa stole them," Molly went on, "and threw them into a talking trash can in the mall."

"The trash can is a kind of lion," I told her.

"But then Hobie rescued them. He snuck into the mall, even though it was strictly forbidden, and to get them back he crawled into Larry Trash Can."

"The kind of lion," I said.

"Are you making this up?" Mrs. Rossi asked.

"They must be worth at least a thousand dollars." Molly reached over and touched one.

"At least," I agreed.

Toby climbed the steps, Fido following him. He'd been listening. "They sparkle," he said. "I'm glad the sharks didn't eat them." His mother let him take the now peeling box, and he shifted it back and forth to make the earring in it flash.

Mrs. Rossi shook her head. "Not a thousand," she said. "More like thirteen."

I almost slid down the steps. Molly gagged. She'd said it would be a lot. But thirteen thousand dollars was more money than I could even think about.

"In truth, it's more," Mrs. Rossi went on. "They cost exactly thirteen dollars and fifty-seven cents."

"They cost what?" Molly grabbed my arm.

"Isn't that a great price?" Mrs. Rossi picked Fido up and chucked her under the chin. "You see, I got them by calling that twenty-four-hour 'Shopping at Home' program on TV. You know the one? They sell lots of gold chains and figurines and music boxes and wrench sets."

We nodded. We knew.

"Well, I saw these earrings one night on TV when everybody else was in bed, and thirteen dollars and fifty-seven cents seemed like such a good price. And then when I called the number, I found out I got five dollars off because I was a first-time shopper. What does that come to?"

"That comes to eight dollars and fifty-seven cents," Molly told her. "Hobie could have gotten thrown out of school and eaten alive by a lion for eight dollars and fifty-seven cents."

"I guess that means they aren't really diamonds, doesn't it?" I asked her.

"You thought they were diamonds? But they're enormous. That's what they're supposed to look like, of course, but real diamonds this size would cost *thousands* of dollars."

Molly groaned.

"What are they? Glass?" I asked her.

"Oh, no. I don't think they'd break if you dropped them, but I expect you couldn't scratch a mirror with them, either. On TV they call them cubic zirconias. It was bargain night on 'Shopping at Home,' and these were such bargains." She fastened the loose earring back in the box. "You know what, though. As soon as I opened them, I knew I couldn't wear them. They'd make me feel like a Christmas tree. Or a chandelier. They're way too flashy. They're not me. They're as big as . . ."

"Jumbo olives," I said.

"Exactly. Jumbo olives. A bargain's not a bargain unless—"

"If you don't want them, can I have them?" Toby asked.

"Well, I don't know. After all, Molly found them in the bush, and Hobie rescued them from the kind of lion," she told him.

"It was nothing," I said.

"Maybe you two would like to have them," Mrs. Rossi suggested, "to remember the storm by?" Molly poked me and nodded.

"Yes, thank you very much," she said. She reached over, took an earring from the box, and clipped it to her right ear. Her head tilted. "I get one for finding them," she told me, "and you get one for saving them."

I picked up the other fake diamond and wiggled it to make it sparkle. It didn't make a bad medal for Bravery in the Mall.

"I did good stuff, too," Toby said. "I didn't cry at all when I heard the gargle monster in the basement, or very much when Hobie fell in the water, and I didn't do you-know-what in my pants even once at the skating rink."

This was true. "Same thing for Darryl," I told him, and I clipped my diamond to the last floppy spike on Darryl's back.

"A taillight," Toby said. "That's good." He smiled up at me. "That's very good."

I was Toby's hero. The kid thought I was terrific. At last I was the dog with the bow tie and the lasso. Fido rubbed against my leg and purred.

"But what do you *say* to Hobie?" Mrs. Rossi asked.

"This earring," Molly moaned, "is so heavy it pinches." She took it off and rubbed her ear. "But of course it won't hurt Darryl. Did you know that stegosauruses were extremely stupid? Their tiny brains were the size of walnuts and weighed only two and a half ounces. My brain, on the other hand, weighs three pounds." Toby stuck out his tongue at her. Fido jumped up and sat in her lap.

"What do you say to Hobie?" Mrs. Rossi asked again. "What are the magic words?"

Toby smiled up at me as if he thought I was wonderful. "You're finished, Scumbreath," he said.

Then he ran out to his new giraffe and sat Darryl in back, his taillight flashing. Settling himself in the driver's seat, he waved goodbye and began to row the air across shark-filled grass to dinosaur land.

Jamie Gilson

says she tries to make her readers "laugh and understand at the same time." She is the author of ten entertaining and popular novels for children, including the four previous Hobie Hanson stories—*Thirteen Ways to Sink a Sub*, *4B Goes Wild*, *Hobie Hanson, You're Weird*, and *Double Dog Dare*, which *Publishers Weekly* called "a worthy lesson, delivered through sparkling dialogue and humorous hijinks."

Ms. Gilson was born in Beardstown, Illinois, and grew up in small midwestern towns where her father was a flour miller. Following graduation from Northwestern University, she taught junior high school students, then wrote for Chicago radio stations WBEZ and WFMT. She has contributed articles to *Chicago* and *Metropolitan Home* magazines and currently conducts writing workshops for sixth graders.

Ms. Gilson and her husband, Jerry, have three children. They live in a suburb of Chicago.